THE DEADLY GAME

THE DEADLY GAME

NORMAN DANIELS

CUTTING EDGE

ISBN-13: 978-1-957868-39-4

Published by
Cutting Edge Books
PO Box 8212
Calabasas, CA 91372
www.cuttingedgebooks.com

CHAPTER ONE

I F I HADN'T been carefully watching Mrs. Luella Cooper, I wouldn't have overheard it, and one of the best chances of my career might have been lost. But I'd hardly taken my eyes off her since I arrived at Jim Fielding's house party.

Fielding was noted for his lavish parties. He always invited just the right number of people so he could personally take care of them all, though he usually made certain there were enough so the guests could pair off. Fielding's house, a three-story affair, was in town, and the top floors were all bedrooms and baths, a fact every amorously inclined man and woman guest had long ago noted.

I knew that Mrs. Cooper's husband was on the Coast on business. In fact, I knew a lot more about Mrs. Cooper than any reliable jeweler should know about any of his clients. My interest in her wasn't amorous, however. What Mrs. Cooper meant to me was a diamond and emerald necklace she liked to flaunt in the faces of her female friends and make them see the emeralds in a greener color than they really were.

I wasn't disappointed when I greeted Mrs. Cooper earlier that evening. She wasn't wearing her necklace, and that suited me fine because lifting a two hundred thousand dollar bit of bric-a-brac off a lady's neck is a pretty difficult feat even under the best conditions. However, I did know she'd been wearing the necklace at a very fancy tea and cocktail party this afternoon and that she had returned to her apartment house much too late to get the thing into her bank vault. Therefore it had to be in her apartment and I thought I knew just about where it was hidden. I wanted that necklace.

So, when Mrs. Cooper gave impressive-looking Jim Fielding a covert little signal, I spotted it. They left the dancing in the gaudy ballroom and went out to a small formal garden at the back of the house—a garden growing mysteriously in the shadows of the skyscrapers and in the cementladen soil of the city. I guessed those blooms must have cost Fielding twenty dollars each, and he could have bought better ones for five dollars a dozen in any florist's shop, but Fielding apparently liked to do things the expensive way.

I saw Fielding take Mrs. Cooper's hand, hold it a moment and then let go and put his arm around her. Jim Fielding's wife was away, as usual, so he had little to worry about. I was wondering if this whole expensive shindig hadn't been arranged just so that Fielding could get together with Mrs. Cooper.

As I said, she wasn't a bad sort. A bit on the snooty side but then, with her dough, she could afford to be. Still she was well built, had a pretty if not beautiful face and at thirty she wasn't too old to take. I had an idea, however, that when you slept with a woman, you shouldn't steal her jewelry.

I trailed them out into the darkness and Fielding took her to one side of the four-car garage. There, in the shadows, he grabbed her and I never heard a whimper from Luella. They were locked together like that for a long time and Fielding's hands and arms wandered all over her and she appeared to enjoy it. That damned gold mesh evening bag with a gold strap dangled from her arm. I wanted that bag as much as Fielding wanted Luella.

I heard Fielding say, "You knew this would happen, my dear. You knew damned well."

"Yes," she replied in a hoarse whisper. "Oh yes, Jim. I've been waiting and waiting. ..."

"Listen," he said, "we can't stay here."

She was silent a moment, then in a low voice she asked the inevitable question. "Where can we go?"

He kissed her a couple of times. Then he said, "You're wonderful. Listen—we'll go back inside and mingle with the guests for a few minutes. Then you drift upstairs." He fumbled in his pocket. "Here is a key. My rooms are at the end of the hall. Let yourself in, put the key on the little table just inside the door and wait for me there."

"Promise you won't be long, Jim."

"No longer than I can possibly help. I'm showing some movies tonight. Nothing sensational, but enough to keep everybody busy for an hour or so."

She said, "Who wants to see movies with you around, darling?"

I got out of there fast and beat them back to the ballroom. Getting my hands on Luella's pet necklace was going to be much easier than I expected.

When they entered the ballroom, I was handy enough so that they both greeted me. Fielding shook hands. "Hello, Mike Sloan," he said. "I saw you around, but I couldn't get near you."

I said, "Good evening, Mr. Fielding. Hello, Mrs. Cooper. You're looking especially lovely."

She nodded rather formally, but her eyes clearly returned the compliment. Even though she intended to hold a tryst with Fielding in just a few minutes, she couldn't resist being interested. That warm, sultry look of hers said that there simply weren't enough men in the world for her.

I saw them separate and Luella was grabbed up for a dance by a bulgy guy with inquisitive paws and an alcohol-glassy pair of eyes. I made my way out of the ballroom, saw nobody around the reception hall and I walked briskly up the curving staircase to the second floor.

Upstairs, some of the bedroom doors were open. A couple were closed, but not empty from the giggling I heard coming through the panels. I proceeded at once to the door of Fielding's rooms that he had told Luella about.

This was an old house, very well kept up and worth a small fortune, but the door locks were the old-fashioned kind which required a long, round key—the easiest sort in the world to pick, and I knew quite a lot about locks. This one surrendered to a special blade on a gold knife I carried. I went inside and snapped on the lights for about ten seconds so that I could spot the location of the furniture and relock the door. Then I put them out, moved a big divan away from the corner and got behind it. I pulled the divan back in place, curled up and waited.

I could visualize that necklace. I'd repaired it several times and the last time I'd worked on it I had learned something particularly intriguing. Some of the diamonds had been a trifle loose and Luella had wanted the whole thing gone over. It had been necessary to clear out a lot of perfumed face powder from under some of the loose gems. She wasn't the first woman to hide her most valuable jewels inside a powder box when they weren't gathering dust in a safe deposit vault.

The necklace was an exquisite piece of yellow gold set with a row of fine diamonds, then a row of emeralds and finally a third row of diamonds. All the stones were perfect, all uniformly large but not so big that they couldn't be easily disposed of. I'd assessed that necklace for two hundred and twenty-five thousand dollars once. I could make a hundred and fifty thousand on it even after I'd broken it up, which I always did with any of the pieces worth going after.

About a dozen of those emeralds could be made up into a neat bracelet, which would look good on Mona's wrist, I thought. Emeralds went with her dark eyes and hair. Having watched Jim Fielding and Luella, and knowing they were coming here soon made me think about Mona. I remembered I had to get her on the phone as quickly as possible when I left this suite of rooms. She was going to have to earn some of those emeralds.

A key slid into the lock, turned and Luella stepped into the room. She snapped on the overhead lights and I automatically ducked lower even though I knew she couldn't see me. Then she lit a dim table lamp and extinguished the others. She put the key on the little table just inside the door and alongside it she placed her gold mesh handbag. I saw that from where I was hidden and I smiled because it was exactly what I knew she'd do.

After five minutes, Fielding showed up. He locked the door and left the key in it. Neither of them said anything. They met in the middle of the room and embraced.

When Fielding, in a thick voice, said, "God, you're beautiful, Luella. You're amazing," I realized she was out of her dress. From my hiding place I could see only their heads.

She was clinging to him, arching back so her body would be pressed tightly against him, and she said, "Jim—let's not hurry back to the party. Those people won't budge while the movies are on. We have plenty of time."

I didn't. Fielding was impatient, for suddenly he curled an arm under her and lifted her. She giggled, threw her arms around his neck, and kicked her legs. He took a couple of steps in the direction of the next room and then he couldn't hold her any longer. He almost dropped her, but she managed to get her feet under her. She started laughing out loud. He stopped that with a hard kiss squarely on her lips, and she grabbed him again.

They disappeared into the next room. After a couple of minutes, there was silence and the light in the other room went out. I waited three minutes by the luminous dial of my watch, climbed over the divan and tiptoed to the door. I picked up her handbag, opened it and found what I was looking for. A single key. I dropped it into my pocket, closed the bag and put it back on the table. I turned the key in the door gently, withdrew it and opened the door a crack. Nobody was in the hall.

I closed the door without making a sound, locked it and put the key in my pocket. Then I started moving fast. The first thing

I did was step into one of the bedrooms, close the door and pick up the telephone. I dialed the office, where Mona always waited when I was on the prowl. She answered right away.

"Listen, baby," I said, "it worked. In ten minutes I'll be in the apartment and out on the street ten minutes after that. That gives you twenty minutes to meet me around the northwest corner of the building. Can do?"

I could almost hear Mona lick her chops. "Can do," she purred. "Good luck, darling."

I went down the stairs. The ballroom was dark and quiet except for the movie screen, on which some fleshy figures cavorted gayly. I slipped out through one of the French doors and nobody would have seen me if I was ten feet tall.

Luella's apartment was in a building only seven blocks north, one of those breaks a guy in my profession hopes for and seldom gets. I whistled for a cab, had myself driven north on the avenue and got off a block beyond the street where Luella lived. I knew every step of the way from here.

The apartment building was provided with a service entrance, a freight elevator which was strictly self-service, and at this hour of the evening there'd be few engineers around. I got into the elevator, sent it to the eleventh floor, walked down two flights and made my way along the corridor to Luella's duplex.

I noticed that the lock in her door looked new and when I thrust her key into it, the whole business operated stiffly. It was a brand new lock, all right, but just about as pickproof as the old one. I didn't turn on any lights, but used the small flat flashlight I carried.

I went through the living room, passed up the dining room and found the stairway to the second floor of the two-story apartment. I knew just where Luella's bedroom was, walked in and sprayed the big French Provincial vanity with light. It had a large metal powder box on it. I put a piece of paper under it, raised the lid and gave a nervous start because opening the lid set off some concealed chimes. They couldn't be heard twenty feet away, but I cursed them anyway. I thrust a finger into the layer of powder and found what I was after with astonishing simplicity. She'd rolled the necklace and a few other bits of jewelry into a piece of wax paper and buried them under the powder. I got them out very carefully, to avoid spilling powder, rolled the jewelry and their wax paper covering into more tissues and put them in my pocket.

I replaced the lid, shook the box to level off the powder inside, cleaned up the vanity, put everything exactly as it was when I came in and wiped away any prints. It was as simple as that. I left by the same route I used to enter, walked casually out the service door to the side street and then stepped briskly to the corner.

As I rounded it, Mona Montinez came out of the shadows. She was wearing an evening gown and a mink jacket over it so that if we were seen, nobody would pay much attention, since we were both formally dressed. Besides, if an emergency compelled her to crash the Fielding party, she'd be prepared. Mona was practical, too.

But being practicad wasn't all there was to Mona. She was tall, only two inches shorter than my six feet, but she wasn't the rangy type. Beautiful as a painting from head to foot, you could see the Spanish background in her family tree. At least she claimed it was Spanish. I went more for the Gypsy idea, possibly because I always was a romantic guy.

She said, "How did it go, darling?"

"Like always," I said. I fished out the tissue-wrapped package and pressed it into her hand. "Unveil it later, baby. Is the car close by?"

She led me to where the club coupé was waiting, and we got in. Mona needed no instructions. She headed straight for Fielding's place. She stopped for a traffic light and leaned over. I kissed her lightly and then seriously. I was still thinking about Fielding and Luella.

"I'll get away early if I can," I said. "Be at the office."

"I'll be there, Mike," she said with a slow smile.

I grinned. "Wait until I tell you what I've been through. No time now. Drop me at the next corner, go back to the office and start work on this stuff."

"Yes, Mike. By the time you get there, I should be almost finished."

She took time to squeeze my knee, and then she was pulling up to the curb. I took a quick look around, slipped out and walked quickly to the driveway beside Fielding's town house. Twenty seconds later I entered through the same French door, right into the same scene I'd left. The movie was still going on.

I went up the stairway, after scanning the faces in the audience as best I could in the gloom. I didn't see Fielding or Luella among them. When I reached the suite, I listened outside the door for half a minute. I also peeked through the old-fashioned keyhole. Only that same weak light was on.

I threaded the key into the lock, turned it carefully, opened the door and listened some more. I could hear Luella speaking in a low voice. I stepped inside, picked up her evening bag and placed the key in it. I laid it down gently, thrust the door key into the lock, turned it and then I stepped softly across the floor, climbed over the divan and crouched down behind it.

I'd had plenty of time, for they didn't come out for another fifteen minutes. Fielding was trying to tie his black tie without a mirror and doing a lousy job of it. Luella picked up her dress and, with one of those deft motions only a woman knows, stepped into it, gave one quick pull and the dress was back in place.

She kissed him once more and then started putting on lipstick. "You're very nice, Jim. Very, very nice."

Fielding wanted to take a couple of minutes for some more necking, which showed he didn't know women as well as he thought he did. Luella's fresh lipstick was on.

Fielding grabbed the doorknob and tried to open the door. He gave a laugh. "I forgot. I locked us in."

I gave them five minutes before I slipped out of the place myself and went downstairs. When the picture was over and the lights went up, I was sitting far back in the room, legs crossed, smoking a cigar and apparently having a hell of a fine time all by myself. I wished Fielding would call it a night because I wanted to get back to Mona—and fast.

CHAPTER TWO

ALTHOUGH I'M IN the retail jewelry business, I don't run a store. I have a very expensive, very fashionable-looking office fitted out with period furniture, a thick rug, a small bar and two elaborate show cases set on especially made tables. My clients expect something in the way of surroundings when they pay me three times what an article is worth.

Behind this office is my workshop, not large but equipped with the finest tools I could buy and a bed-divan where I often spend the night when I am exceptionally busy or—when Mona is with me.

Mona had taken off her evening gown and was wearing a plastic apron over her slip as she perched on the high stool at the workbench. She certainly had wonderful legs, and they were prominently on display right now. All she did was look up, smile once and then she was back at work. I peeled off my coat, rolled up my sleeves and found she had the smelting furnace going good. The gold portions of Luella's jewelry lay in a heap, stripped of the gems. I put the stuff into a crucible, lifted it into the electric furnace with a pair of tongs, closed the door and checked the time.

Mona was sorting the diamonds according to size and studying each one for any secret marks. She found a few and put these to one side. I pulled over another high stool, screwed a jeweler's loupe in my right eye and began double checking the gems.

They were of fine quality, fiery and alive. There wasn't a dud in the lot of them and the emeralds were of equal quality. I swept

THE DEADLY GAME

the handful of diamonds into the palm of my left hand, carried them out to the main office and unlocked the big vault. I opened the door and pulled out a tray lined with black velvet and containing a couple of hundred fine diamonds. I let those that had belonged to Luella trickle through my fingers. Nobody on earth could tell her stones from mine now, and I could even furnish bills of sale to account for the ones I'd just added.

Mona touched my shoulder. I knew what she wanted. I closed the tray and pulled another one out containing emeralds. She was set to drop Luella's green gems in with the others, but I stopped her by grabbing her wrist, squeezing it just a little until her fingers opened and revealed the stones she was holding. I picked out a dozen of them—all of excellent quality.

"Okay, hon," I said. "Put the others down."

She dumped them into the tray. I closed and locked the safe and then handed her the dozen I'd saved out. "I'll turn these into a bracelet for you."

Her fingers closed around the jewels. "Mike, do you mean that? Why these are worth ..."

"Damned little compared to what I owe you. Come on, Mona."

I took her wrist and led her back into the workroom. On the way she dropped the emeralds on the bench. I sat down on the divan, pulled her onto my lap and kissed her. Then I relaxed.

Mona didn't. Her breasts rose and fell fast, and her eyes were smoky black now.

I said, "Baby, what kind of a guy am I? Just how do you think of me?"

"A swell guy, Mike. A swell guy and the best damn jewel thief in history."

I nodded. "A few other people are saying the same thing."

"Well," she said, "you rate the praise, don't you?"

"Not people in the profession. People like Captain Kane. When a cop like Kane begins talking too much, he's either gone soft or he's ready to put the skids under you, and Kane is not soft-headed."

Mona put a finger under my chin and gazed at me. "Poor Mike," she said. "You're stewing again. Listen, darling, you're more than just a good crook. You're an expert, and beyond that you happen to own a legitimate business which gives you a good living without the other."

"Then why in hell don't I stick to it instead of taking all these crazy risks?"

"Because you like excitement. You like exciting things— exciting women …."

I pulled off the clammy plastic apron she was still wearing. "I like your kind of exciting woman. But how much longer can I hope to get away with this racket? This double life? I've got a feeling they're closing in."

"Nonsense. They may suspect, but there is no proof. Let them close in."

"They'll grab you too, sweetie."

"I'm not worried about that, but if you are, Mike, why don't you quit?"

I laughed, but it had a hollow ring to it. "The first time I swiped anything, I told myself it would be just one job to get me started. Then I saw some snob of a woman with a fortune around her neck and there was one more job. It keeps on that way. I can't stop."

She snuggled further down on my lap. "Then why try, Mike? So long as things go right, take what you want. If you get too much stashed away, little Mona won't turn down some of it."

"You'll get your share, beautiful, don't worry."

"I'm not." Her enormous black eyes were shining into mine. "I didn't mean that crack. You've paid me off better than I deserve for the small part I play in this business. You ought to be proud, Mike. Proud of your work. You never hurt anyone except in their pocketbooks, and most of those fat bitches can afford it. You've never made a mistake, you have the right setup here. You're accepted socially and most of your friends are influential people."

"I know, baby. But—"

"You've got to forget about Captain Kane."

"Make me, Mona. Make me forget."

She moved her face toward mine, and then I saw her nostrils flare out. She slipped off my lap. "The damn furnace," she exclaimed.

It was stinking up the whole workshop. I hurried over to it, shut the thing off and took out the crucible with tongs. I poured the molten gold into toy-sized ingot molds. In my vault I had a hundred ingots just like these—all imprinted with the name of a legal gold supply house just as these new ones would be marked.

Mona filled the sink with water. I carried the molds over and dunked them until they were cool enough to handle. We slipped them out of the molds then, hid the molds and carried the ingots out to the main office and the vault. I put them with the others. If anybody cared to check, I had more papers to prove I'd bought these fresh ingots legally.

I turned out the lights and went back to the workshop. I left the furnace door open so it would cool, for if Captain Kane had somehow learned of the latest job and came calling, he'd wonder why I was running a furnace at this hour of the morning. So I put out all the lights except one in the workshop. If he came now, he could knock until his knuckles got blue.

I went over to the divan where Mona was waiting for me. She was stretched out on it, but she made room for me and I sat down so I could bend over and kiss her easily.

"Do you think Kane really has something on you?"

"He can't have. I never left anything for him to find."

"But in all these big jobs you're the common denominator. You're the one person who knows all the victims. You also knew they had those pieces of jewelry. Sometimes you even sold the

NORMAN DANIELS

stuff and then swiped it back. That's why Kane wonders about you. There's nothing else, Mike. No tangible thing, I mean."

I got an arm under her shoulders. She smiled languidly and reached up for me. "Your big trouble is lack of confidence, darling."

"Yeah," I said glumly. "Everything sounds nice except that one word 'thief.' I've never been able to take any pride in that."

"Then why did you get into this business, Mike?"

"I don't know—exactly. I suppose I like gems. They fascinate me—like women. Each is different. Each has its own individual coloring and shape. It can be a glittering thing full of fire or it can be cold and forbidding. Oh, that's nonsense. I like gems because they bring me money. Lots of money."

"And why, darling? You tear those beautiful creations to bits, melt the gold, sell the gems individually and make sixty to seventy percent of the actual worth. That's what makes you so successful—and rich."

I nodded. "Yeah—I've got a roll. And if I'm thrown into prison, I'll still be rich when I get out. But when am I going to realize that I have enough? That's what I ask myself. I used to say all I needed was to put my business in sound shape. That was easy, but I wanted a little more. Now I can't stop. I like the devil's ways, but I don't want to pay up."

She tugged with both hands and I bent over her. "Mike," she said, "you wanted me to make you forget. Kiss me."

This made me think of Fielding and Luella. I suddenly fastened my lips against hers and held them there. Her grip became tighter, her lips parted under mine and her breasts pressed harder against my chest. She was so easily mine whenever I wanted her and yet for me genuine passion just wasn't there. I knew it.

I was an idiot, prowling the darkness that was my future, in search of someone to excel Mona. And where would I find such a woman? She'd have to possess this wonderful body, surpass the exciting beauty of this oval face with its olive skin and black eyes.

14

She'd have to match Mona's vitality and responsiveness and go even further. Such a woman didn't exist. Yet I kept craving her.

Mona was saying something and I had to ask her what she had said.

"Damn you, Mike. You go off into some kind of a crazy dreamland and you pick the God-damnedest times to do it. I swear sometime I'll just leave you flat. You deserve it."

"I'm sorry, Mona. I was thinking back to make sure I hadn't muffed anything."

Any ordinary girl would have pouted about playing second fiddle to business but not Mona. She smiled. "Well, that's different, darling. For a second there, I thought you had some other girl on your mind."

"I know no other girls. I haven't since I met you."

She murmured something warm and happy. She curled closer against me. Only the swinging lamp over the workbench was on, and it hardly reached us over against the wall where the divan was. There was only enough light to make her skin shine like a jewel. That's what Mona was—a gem. A perfect, flawless gem. She was something like the legend of the pearl. It comes from the sea a cold, lifeless thing, but placed next to a woman's skin it becomes alive. Mona was exactly like that. She'd been cold and distant at first. But now she was the pearl against the warmth of skin. I thought, somewhat crazily, that if I laid a string of virgin pearls against her skin right now, they'd probably burn up.

She wasn't talking any more and neither was I. We were both warm and content—together. Some day I'd marry this girl. I told myself that two or three times a week. But I knew it was a lie. For I was waiting for something. Someone would come along one day and Mona would mean nothing. I think she sensed it too but, like me, she was willing to gamble with the future and wanted to get all there was out of the present.

I finally got up and turned off the work light.

CHAPTER THREE

AT TEN THE next morning a buzzer under my desk hissed twice. That meant Mona, in the reception office, was signaling trouble. I opened the lacquered cigarette box on my desk, tapped a butt, lit it and leaned back. Usually Mona announced visitors and clients, but Captain Jack Kane didn't believe in being announced. He flung the door wide open, as he always did—like he figured there might be someone hiding behind it. He was a big, burly man. Not quite as tall as me, but heavier and a lot more rugged. His hair was mouse-colored; he had a very usual face; he had ten fingers and probably ten toes. He was manifestly normal in all departments that I could see except his eyes—and there was the difference. I'd never seen such colorless eyes in my life. Being a jeweler, they naturally put me in mind of some hard gemlike substance, the name of which evaded me. So I settled for glass—or ice—which described both their color and coldness. And whatever lights glinted there were reflected brilliance. Those eyes had no inner life of their own. Looking him square in the face now, I could see that the fire of anger had struck light to it. But it was not the kind of anger one expects to find on the face of an honest cop, outraged on behalf of the citizenry to be protected. His face was alive with personal hatred, and the glitter in those ice eyes was the glitter of—could it be greed? I put my feet on the desk, something I never did except when Kane blustered in here on some kind of wild hunch, his strong-arm tactics flexed like a carnival Samson's muscles. Over his shoulder I could see Mona nodding at me almost imperceptibly. This meant someone was with him and, according to Mona's code, a lot more trouble. "What's new, friend?" I inquired in a lazy casual voice.

This made him as furious as I thought it would, and to prove it he slammed the door. Then he strode across the office and leaned over my desk. "Not long ago," he said, "somebody entered the apartment of Luella Cooper. I don't suppose you ever heard of her."

"Heard of her?" I echoed placidly, ignoring his threatening manner. "Of course. As a matter of fact, Mrs. Cooper is a valued customer of mine. And she is also a very popular hostess, so I'm not surprised that 'somebody,' as you say, 'entered' her apartment."

"Very cute, very cute," he told me. "I suppose you know she lost her diamond and emerald necklace—if 'lost' is the word."

"Not surprised," I said. "I knew she would." And I gave Kane a straightforward innocent look, right into his pretty ice eyes.

This brought a great boom of derision from him, like a chemical explosion. "You're not surprised? I'll say you weren't! You've been scheming to grab that necklace ever since you knew it existed!"

"I like lovely things, Kane," I said. "Why don't you frisk me?"

I thought he was going to kick me instead, but he evidently thought better of it, and after a moment's visible calculation, he drew up a chair with one of his paws, and looked even more like a trained bear when he sat down on it. "Maybe we can have a little talk," he began. "Like—where were you night before last?"

This brought him a big broad smile as a special present from me. I couldn't help it. He was as adept at the detecting business as a tourist making conversation with the aid of a phrase book is in a foreign language. "Aren't you wasting our time, Captain?" I asked. "Are you sure it's night before last you want to know about? Or isn't that just the wind-up gimmick you're trying to use to confuse me and make me louse up my alibi for the night you're really interested in? Okay," I hurried on before he could stop me, "if you're really so keen on my exciting daily adventures I'll spill all, just like you were. Dear Diary. Night before last I worked in my shop back of the office until very late. Nobody saw me. I signed the lobby book when I left, but not when I arrived because I just stayed right on here without going anywhere. I don't think anyone saw me leave. You know how deserted these office buildings are at two-thirty in the morning."

"Then you have no alibi?" He acted as if it were important.

"Not for the night before last."

"You went home at two-thirty, you say?"

"That's right."

"And went to bed?"

"I was dead tired. Had to make up a very special brooch for Mrs. Oliver Lane's fiftieth wedding anniversary. Lots of fancy designing and gem setting. Wore me down."

"What time did you get back to the office yesterday?"

"About noon. Mona takes care of the place very well when I'm not here."

"Mona could take care of anything well," Kane said and there was a nasty, suggestive twist to the way he said it.

I gave him a genial grin instead of a right to the jaw. "I presume you want to know about my activities right up until now. Well, yesterday afternoon I stayed in the office. I can prove that for several clients were here. I went home at six, had dinner in the dining room of my hotel, dressed and went to a party thrown by Jim Fielding. There must have been thirty people there, so I can prove that, too."

"When did you leave?"

"Approximately one in the morning. I went home, had some sleep and came down here this morning. That brings us up to the present moment."

Kane stood up importantly. Here came the interrogation. "You never left Fielding's party at all?"

"No. It was an interesting party. He showed some movies which—well, they wouldn't interest a policeman who sees all sides of life. No, they wouldn't interest you—much."

"I heard they were pornographic films."

"That all depends on how your mind works. I just thought they were dirty."

"But you sat through them?"

"Why not? I was a guest, and I knew beforehand what Fielding's idea of entertainment is. Sure I stayed."

Finally Kane sat down again. I was sick of having him tower over me, and I was damned if I'd be courteous to him. He shoved his hat to the back of his head tough-copper fashion and glared at me.

"Sloan, you're slick. Let me assure you I know that. I've been a cop for a lot of years. I've worked on plenty of jewel robbery cases. I know the local Gold Coast better than a politician knows his own ward. I've seen crooks come and go. I've seen them all—from George Field, who we think swiped about a million dollars worth of furs and gems, to Julia Abortofsky, the hotel maid who lifted a fortune."

"What are you driving at, Kane?"

"Just this, smart boy. People think jewel thieves are slim, gentlemanly guys with wispy mustaches, manicured finger-nails, nice manners and a gift of gab. People are all wrong. Jewel thieves are plain, lousy, goddam crooks just like the lug who saps some sucker with a tire iron and rolls him. They're in the same class with a jack-roller who specializes in drunks. Every one of them—and this includes you—are dumb punks with no fancy trimmings."

I said, "I admire your eloquence. Now tell me about the one who was different."

"You mean Gerard Dennis." He continued like a straight man. "Sure, they had him down on the books as a gent. Well, maybe he did have more brains than the average mug, but he swiped half a million bucks and what did he do with it? Threw it away on women, got himself caught through one of them and where is he now? In stir."

I put a puzzled frown on my face. "I still don't know what you're driving at, Jack."

"Which proves you're a stupid jerk just like all other crooks. Listen, Mike, this setup—" He waved his hand at the office— "doesn't fool me one bit. Neither does that flashy broad in the front office nor the two hundred dollar suits you wear. You're a punk and you always will be."

I took my feet off the desk. "I resent the fact that you called Miss Montinez a broad. As for the rest of it, I'd like to call in a witness and have you repeat it all. Let's see you do that, Kane. Go ahead—back yourself up."

"You'd sue the pants off me," he said with a growl. "And maybe get away with it too, because people are dopes. Especially people on juries. I'm not falling into that trap."

"Then stop calling me names and get down to facts. If I'm supposed to have robbed somebody, tell me about it and I'll try to prove I didn't. Otherwise you can do one of two things. Get the hell out of my office or arrest me."

He took a black cigar from his pocket. It was a cheap one, without cellophane; some of the dark wrapper had peeled off. He licked the whole thing like a dog licking an ice cream cone, bit off the end and pursed his lips as if to spit it out on my floor. I made a few noises in my throat. He behaved himself, simply lit up and smoked.

"Last night," he went on. "Somebody did get Mrs. Cooper's necklace, along with a couple of other doodads. If she'd been a reasonable woman, it wouldn't have happened. I wanted to put a man on her tail, but she refused pointblank."

I thought I knew the reason why—Jim Fielding. "Mrs. Cooper was at the party last night and she wasn't wearing her necklace. I'm sure of that," I said.

"No, she didn't wear it. She left it at home—hidden, she says. I'd done what I could. I knew she'd seen you and you'd handled the necklace. I persuaded her to let me put a new lock on her door, and there was only one key to it. Just one, Sloan, and she carried it with her. She had it last night at the party you both attended."

"All right," I said. "She had a key. So what?"

"So somebody opened that lock with a key. Let me repeat—there was only one and she didn't have it long enough for a duplicate to be made."

I let out a curt laugh. "Kane, you've been a cop too long. You're getting dull-witted. There are guys who can open any lock, most of them with a hairpin."

"Not this one—or at least we'd have known if it was picked. Her key was used."

"Did she say I took the key?"

"She did not—yet. But she's outside, and we're going to thrash this out now. If I find you came close enough to her to swipe that key, I'll jug you, Mike. I swear I will."

"Bring her in," I invited, wondering what he thought this would prove. Perhaps in his simple dumb way he thought I'd break down when confronted by her. Mrs. Cooper was undoubtedly the danger Mona had signaled about.

Kane went to the door, opened it and beckoned to her. She wasn't too eager. I arose and offered her my hand. "I'm sorry about the necklace, Mrs. Cooper. It seems that Captain Kane has a slightly exaggerated idea that I stole it."

"You, Mr. Sloan?" she gasped. "But really, I made no such accusation."

Kane said, "He knows that, Mrs. Cooper. You understand we have to follow all the leads. Now we know your apartment door was opened with your key. It had to be. There just wasn't any other way to get in. Sloan, here, knew you owned the necklace, knew its value. He was also at Fielding's party last night, and it's conceivable he could have had something to do with it."

"But Captain Kane," she protested. "Why, I've known Mr. Sloan a long time. He's had the necklace more than once—had it for a couple of days. If he's a thief, why didn't he steal it then?"

Kane said, "Look, Mrs. Cooper, I'm not accusing him. I did not say, at any time, that Sloan is a thief. I only want to know if it was possible that he could have sneaked that key away from you."

She looked at Kane, then at me and then back at Kane again. She was confused—and with good reason.

I said, "Mrs. Cooper, the Captain might be a trifle crude in the way he puts his questions. Let me try it. Where did you keep the key?"

"Why—in my evening bag."

"I see. Now did you put me in possession of that evening bag at any time last night?"

"Of course not."

"Did you at any time put it down? So that I might have—shall we say—opened it?"

She hesitated. "Why, I … that is …"

Kane never was the patient type. "Did you or did you not put that bag down last night? At any time?"

"No," she said. "No, I did not."

I said, "There you are, Captain. Is there anything else?"

"No," he said curtly and angrily. "All right, Mrs. Cooper, I'll be with you in a minute."

She walked to the door and turned her head around before she opened it. She gave me an inquisitive and doubtful look. Then she went out.

Kane towered over me again. "You're a smart cookie, Mike. Some day I'll find out how you lifted that key. It'll get me a promotion, but more than that it'll stick you in a cell where you belong. Remember what I said—a jewel thief is no different from any other crook. He always makes a slip. When you do, I'll be waiting and in the meantime I'll make life as miserable for you as I possibly can."

If I'd made up my mind never to pull another job, I would have changed it then just to show up this stupid bastard.

He waited to see if I'd make some crack. I didn't—I just ignored him and pretended large preoccupation with a pile of letters on my desk. He slammed the door again when he left. I stayed with the mail.

Mona came in soon afterwards and she looked worried.

"Kane bothers me, Mike. He's too damned persistent. He comes here after every job that's pulled, whether it's yours or not."

"Let him be, baby. So long as he can't get anything on me, we're having the fun, not him."

"But it's getting too dangerous. Suppose Mrs. Cooper had put her evening bag down where you might have picked it up ...."

"She did, sweetheart. How else could I have borrowed the key? But right after she put it down, she went to bed with our host, and I don't think Mrs. Cooper would like to admit that."

"Then do you think she might suspect?"

"Who cares? There isn't a thing she can do about it. Stop worrying, Mona, for God's sake. We're in the clear and you'll feel better if you remember that."

"Yes, Mike. But I've been thinking." She paused, then added, "Look, Mike, promise me you'll lay off for a while. We've got enough legitimate business to carry us. It could even grow if you paid more attention to it."

I said, "Sure, we'll lay low."

She hoisted herself up to the edge of the desk. "I don't like the way you just said that—nor the gleam in your eyes. Mike, have you another job planned?"

I said, "Okay, maybe I have. First, go out front and select a necklace. Any kind you like and put it on. I want to try something."

She didn't seem too keen on the idea, but her curiosity was aroused and she went out. I opened a desk drawer and took out a slim, rodlike tool that I thrust under my shirt, next to my skin, and held there with an elbow. Then I turned on the small radio we use for news flashes, tuned in on a dance band, and when Mona came in, I saw that she wore a single strand, pearl necklace. That suited me fine.

"Now what happens?" she asked.

"The music," I said, "is perfect for dancing and I haven't danced with you in a long time. Besides, you're jittery and dancing is good for the nerves."

Before she could protest, I had her in my arms and moved her across the floor. After a little bit, she stopped being stiff and fell naturally into the rhythm and my lead. Mona was a first-rate dancer, responsive and soft.

We continued until the record was over and the announcer started a commercial. I walked around and sat down behind my desk. Mona stood facing me.

"I still don't get it, darling. I was to put on a necklace—"

"What necklace?" I asked with a straight face.

Her fingers flew to her throat. The necklace was, of course, gone. For a moment she went white and then started looking around the floor. Then she heard me laughing. I stuck out my hand, opened the fingers and showed her the pearls.

"Are you looking for these, baby?"

The color rushed back to her cheeks. "Damn you, Mike, you lifted those—"

"And you never knew it. You felt absolutely nothing."

"But, Mike—how?"

I showed her the rod-like instrument I'd dreamed up quite a while before and had finally perfected.

"With—that?" she asked in considerable awe.

I showed her how it worked. "A touch at the base sends up a clipper that could cut through steel as if it were cheese. Now look on either side of the tiny clipper. See that tiny pincer-like hook? What's the greatest danger in stealing a necklace off a woman's neck without her knowing it? The fear of dropping it. With this hook you can't. All I have to do is maneuver the lady to a point where nobody can see me operate. Then, in less than three or four seconds, I have the necklace off and in my pocket."

She wanted to handle the instrument, so I gave it to her. She tried it out, marveling at its efficiency.

I said, "Another small item not to be overlooked. That gadget has to be carried next to the skin for a long enough period to make it warm with body heat. Then, if I touch the victim's neck, she doesn't feel any metallic cold. You didn't feel a thing, Mona, and yet I touched your neck with it—deliberately."

"Mike, this is wonderful. You could even make this thing look like a metal pencil. Just slip the tip off when you want to use it."

I nodded. "I wondered if you'd come up with something like that. It's a great idea and I'll get to work on it. There's plenty of time before I'll want to use it."

She said, "Then you do have a certain job in mind?"

"Of course. Did you think I'd sit still just because of Kane? Mona, I'm going after the Brindley pearls."

"Captain Kane probably knows you had them in here for cleaning and restringing, Mike. He'll have those pearls watched like the crown jewels."

"Do you think he could catch me removing them? Honestly now, Mona. With the use of this instrument do you believe Kane would know?"

"Probably not, and Mrs. Brindley wouldn't even miss them for hours, but count me out."

"Mona, I never thought you'd get cold feet."

"Uh-uh, darling. Not cold feet. Cold heart—because I still think this is too dangerous. I don't want you to pull it."

I rolled the instrument in a piece of flannel cloth and stowed it away in my desk. "I have to, baby," I said. "I want to. Mrs. Brindley takes that necklace out of the bank once or twice a year. She'll wear it at the Fairweather Ball, and that comes off in two weeks. I've already been invited."

"Captain Kane will have that affair covered as airtight as a plastic bag."

"I can handle it, baby," I said again.

Mona came around behind the desk. "You know how I feel, Mike. I'm just worried, that's all. Kane's getting too close."

"So are you, baby," I said reaching for her. "Remember these are business hours."

CHAPTER FOUR

I T'S MY NATURE never to worry, so that's perhaps why I grossly underestimated Captain Kane. I began finding out what he could do a couple of days later. First of all, diamond merchants don't just go out and buy stones when and where they want to. Diamonds are a tightly controlled commodity under a strictly closed corporation. Fresh stones are sold only once or twice a year, at what is known as a diamond auction to which you have to be invited. No invitation, no bidding. I'd come a good distance in the past three years and I'd been buying special diamonds as a matter of course. I was all set for the auction and when an invitation didn't arrive, I thought it was just an oversight and I called up the secretary to get one.

I was told, rather coldly, that my name wasn't on the list and it was not an oversight. There was nothing I could do. Of course this couldn't stop me from getting diamonds. I could purchase them from men who did attend the auction, but I wouldn't have my pick and I'd have to pay the buyer a profit besides.

That Kane could be responsible for this seemed awfully remote, so I just put it down to the stupidity of somebody connected with the monopoly. However, a few days later I tried to get credit from a bank and was turned down even though my credit standing was tops. They said something about risks involved with gem merchants in these days of crazy taxes and inflation. I got the money from another bank where I'd never done any business before, but I had to put up some of my personal securities to get it. Still I didn't connect Kane with my troubles.

I first became suspicious when I visited old Marty Carroll and tried to dispose of some of the surplus stones I'd accumulated over a period of time. Marty knew they were stolen, but they were not at all heated up with publicity or even recognizable as loot from a job.

Marty said, "I'm sorry, Mike. You just got yourself in wrong lately. Don't ask me any questions and don't come here any more. It ain't that I don't like you or the kind of business you bring, but the pressure—you know how it is."

This really made me hot. I slammed out of his shop. The cops knew what Marty was even though they'd never proven anything, and yet they could scare him like this. It had to be Kane's work. I could almost smell it. Just to make certain, I went around to one of the fancy hotels and called Ernest Haver's suite, toting my anger like a ball and chain.

Haver was a fingerman. He wasn't a thief himself, but he would set the stage for the actual crook and he'd helped me a couple of times. Haver maintained a spot in society where he was accepted everywhere and believed to be a personable young man of pleasant character and with money from the estate of a remote relative. With Ernie Haver, a crook paid off handsomely because he was always worth his big cut. I had feathered his nest plenty.

Haver said, "Oh, it's you, Mike. I'm sorry, but you can't come up. I—I've got someone with me . . . ."

I dropped the phone on the hook in the lobby booth, boarded an elevator and in a few seconds I was hammering on Ernie's door. I said, "Open up, Ernie, or I'll cave the door in. I mean it."

He must have believed me because he opened up while my hand was still on the door. Ernie was in an opulent dressing gown and he wore a highball in his left fist.

He said, "Mike, I told you . . . ."

I strolled past him and investigated the other two rooms of his suite. There was nobody with him. I came back to the living room and fixed myself a drink from his bar. Then I sat down.

"What's the matter, Ernie?" I asked. "Don't you think I can take bad news?"

He shrugged. "I said I was sorry, Mike. I am."

"Who rolled out a blackball for me, Ernie?"

"Mike, you know how it is …"

"Who, Ernie? Who?"

"Nobody. That is—well …"

I tilted the glass, drank the whole highball down and then put the glass on the table. I got up and walked over to where he was sitting. Ernie looked the part he acted. A thin guy with a thin mustache, a rather undeveloped chin, but handsome in spite of it. He looked like a guy who could energetically play-boy all day and night, but I knew his greatest amount of exercise came from lifting and putting down a glass.

I grabbed him by the lapels of his dressing gown, hauled him to his feet and pulled his face to within a couple of inches of mine.

"I asked you a question, Ernie. All over town I'm losing contacts. Not because of anything I've done, but because of pressure. I think I know who is turning the screws, but I want to be sure. So I'm asking you again."

He tried to pull free of my grasp. "Mike, I can't …" he whined.

I let go of him with my right hand, slapped him hard and slapped him again. "I can keep this up a long time, pal. I hate to do it, but I can. Tell me who did this and I promise not to come back."

"God damn you, Mike," he whimpered.

I slapped him half a dozen more times and I was just getting ready to use knuckles on him when he broke.

"It was Captain Kane—you knew that Let go of me, Mike. I'm not the kind of a guy who wants to hate you."

I let go of him. "To hell with you, Ernie. I don't need you."

I jammed on my hat and walked out. I didn't know what to do with myself and, as usual, I gravitated toward Mona's apartment. I wasn't looking for any consolation or forgetfulness tonight. All I wanted was someone to talk to, and Mona could be a fine listener.

She listened now. I was half aware that the gown she wore was low, but so were my spirits just then. I started getting my troubles off my mind.

"Kane has gone too far, baby. He's blackballed me with the diamond syndicate auctions, with banks I usually do business with. He's intimidated a guy who buys my surplus stuff and he put his own dirty thumb on the best fingerman in the business. Ernie Haver told me it was Kane."

"I knew it," Mona said. "I was sure Kane would do something like that."

"He won't stop me," I said.

Mona stuck a cigarette between her lips, but had difficulty lighting it with hands that shook too much. I snapped on my lighter and held it for her.

"Mike, if he's gone to all that trouble, he's gone further. I'm betting you're being tailed around the clock."

I hadn't thought of that; there hadn't been time. Now that I did I didn't like the idea. It was more than possible however. Once the Robbery Detail decides a man is a thief, they'll spend weeks just following him around.

I had a cigarette of my own. I blew smoke toward the ceiling and followed it with my eyes. I said, "I wonder if Kane ever slipped somewhere along the line. A man who works as he does is capable of snide tricks and maybe a little larceny on the side."

Mona was plainly afraid now. "Mike, don't be a fool. Don't try to corner him. Lay low for a while. Kane will cool off if you don't give him any reasons to stay hot on you."

"I need the moral reassurance of knowing I can get Kane, and I will."

She came over and knelt in front of my chair, put her head on my knees and spoke in a low begging voice. "Mike, don't. Forget the whole thing and especially forget the Brindley necklace. Kane is capable of framing you if there is no other way. I've known men like him. They never stop."

"Neither do I, Mona, and Kane will have to get smarter than he is to pull a frame on me."

She wound her arms around my neck. "Can't you see, Mike? It's you I'm thinking of. If they catch you, I'll—I'll—"

"But if Kane has slipped somewhere, and I repeat, he's the kind of a louse who might have—then I can make the son-of-a-bitch pull in his neck and stop bothering me."

"But how do you know he isn't perfectly honest, Mike?"

"Call it a hunch. Call it more than that. Look how he's ganging up on me! Do ordinary cops operate that way? Hell, they go after a man straight. Kane's using influence to get at me."

"Mike, it might be that he's driving you to desperation so you won't be so careful the next time you pull a job. That's all he's waiting for—just a little carelessness on your part. Kane regards you as his personal problem. You've driven him nuts a few times, and he can't forget it."

"Look, baby, will you help me with this?"

She got off my lap quickly. "Nothing doing, Mike. And I'm thinking more of your own good than mine. Kane is just waiting to pounce."

"Take it easy. I don't mean helping me pull a job. All I want you to do is nose around and see what Kane does in his spare time."

She lit another cigarette. Her hands weren't shaking quite as badly this time. "Mike—I'll do that much for you. Maybe I can convince you that Kane is on the level and you can't get at him this way. If I do, will you promise to lay low?"

"It's a promise," I said. I got up too and walked toward her. She came into my arms willingly enough. I hadn't been in the mood when I arrived but, as it usually happened, I couldn't be with Mona long before the fires started leaping.

She pushed me away. "Not tonight, Mike. I'm too worried."

"Oh hell, is Kane getting at me through you, too?"

"Let me check up on him, darling. If I can put my mind at ease, then I'll stop this stewing. Damn it, right now I'd like to get drunk."

"What a lovely idea," I said.

"Oh, no. If I did, I know what would happen. Go home, Mike. Go home and do some serious thinking about this."

I let go of her and found my hat.

She followed me to the door. "Mike, you're not sore at me?"

"No—I realize you have a point, but you worry too much. Take tomorrow off and see what you can find out about Kane. I'll see you tomorrow night."

She gave me a hasty kiss and I didn't find much consolation in it. Without even trying, Kane was getting at me in a way he never planned on. Mona was essential to my plans, but if she was getting the jitters, I'd never be able to use her. I damned Kane a thousand times and kept right on damning him when I hit the street and caught a glimpse of the young dick who fell in half a block behind me.

I took him for a walk and a dozen blocks further on, he faded out of sight and another man took his place. These robbery detail dicks sometimes worked as many as twelve men around the clock to keep a suspect under close surveillance.

I couldn't operate if they watched me that way. Besides, it irritated me. I had to do something about those shadows and I had to do it right away. I headed toward my hotel and I could almost hear the gasp of relief the guy behind me uttered. I took away that relief by going right past the hotel entrance. I walked around the block, studying a neighborhood I'd lived in for five years and had never really seen before. My suite, on the eighth floor, had a rear exposure and I had a recollection of noticing a smaller hotel on the next block. I saw it now from the street. It wasn't a new hotel, but not too bad either.

I circled the block and walked into my own hotel, went straight to my rooms and fixed a drink. Then I sat down to do some planning. First of all, I had to get Kane's boys out of my hair and I didn't think that would be very hard.

I waited until around two in the morning and then I walked down to the lobby floor. At this hour the place was usually deserted, but I caught a glimpse of a bored man dozing in a chair that faced the elevators. That would be Kane's boy. I made sure he didn't see me.

The porter's baggage room was at the rear of the lobby floor and unmanned after midnight so I had no trouble crossing to a small door which led to a loading platform. Now I was in the court behind the hotel. I waited a couple of minutes until my eyes got used to the gloom and then I walked toward the solid wooden fence bordering the edge of the hotel property. It was easy to climb and I found myself in another small court. From this I could reach an alley, go along that to the street and when I did, I found myself face to face with the small hotel I'd already cased. So my idea would work out—if I needed it.

I returned to my hotel by the same route. Kane's man was still dozing. I was tempted to walk past just to see him jump, but I restrained myself and took the elevator to my rooms. I went straight to bed and thought about Mona. I thought so much about her that it took me a long time to drop off.

CHAPTER FIVE

I MISSED HER the next morning when I reached the office. The mail was spilled over the floor below the door slot. I picked it all up, went into my private office and sorted the envelopes. There were two letters from clients who had retained me to look for certain items and each customer cancelled the order. The loss in money wasn't too bad, but it seemed like more of Kane's work.

Up to the time Mona arrived at four in the afternoon, I hadn't had a single customer. Some days were like that because I had a limited amount of business, but I was wondering if Kane had posted men outside to steer customers away. I wouldn't put it past him. Maybe Mona was right and he'd try to drive me into desperate circumstances. What Kane didn't know about was that I could hold out longer than he.

Mona was tired and depressed when she finally turned up. She flung herself into the big leather chair at the side of my desk, slipped off her gloves and gratefully accepted the cigarette I handed her.

"Well," she said, "I checked and I checked. I found out a few things, none of them worth much. Kane likes a good time and spends more than his salary. He also likes beautiful women even though he has a very pretty wife. He has a bad credit rating, and his buying habits indicate he spends a lot on himself and nothing on his house or wife. All in all, I'd say Kane was a louse—but an honest louse. He's never gone off the beam that I could learn."

I felt more than pleased. "You did well, baby. If Kane hasn't strayed, he will. Under a setup like that, a cop is a pushover for the first good deal that comes along. And if nothing does, I'll arrange something."

"And what, for instance?"

"I don't know yet. Maybe I'll do it through his wife."

Mona sat up very straight. "I won't stand for any two-timing on your part, Mike. I'm warning you."

I laughed at her. "Don't worry about it, Mona."

She relaxed. "But Mike, the more I learned about Kane, the more I know how dangerous he is. Remember those Sutton Place jobs a year ago? Movie actresses, a skating star, rich oil men from Texas—nearly half a million was lifted from their apartments. Kane worked on that. He worked around the clock for months and he landed the thieves. He never gives up, and you're top man on his list."

"I'm peeling myself off the top, baby. I'll start tonight. You go home and take it easy. I'll see you later—as soon as I get a definite line on what I want to do about Kane."

I stuck around the office until seven and then I went to a good restaurant in the neighborhood. I bought a newspaper on my way, and I didn't even try to check on Kane's boys, who would be following me. I ate a leisurely dinner, consulted the timetable of a big movie house close by and noted that the feature went on at eight-forty-two. That meant a lot of people would be streaming out about then.

At exactly eight-forty I bought a logs ticket and walked casually across the massive foyer. The early show audience was already coming out of half a dozen lobby doors. I surrendered my ticket, walked in, picked up speed and joined the crowd waiting to go out. I used the far door and made sure there were plenty of people all around me. I kept pace with them until we hit the street. I turned left, walked a dozen yards and popped into a large drug store. I went straight to the phone booths, entered one of them and kept my eyes peeled for anyone who resembled a cop. Nobody gave me even a casual glance.

After five minutes of pretended telephoning, I left the drug store by the side door which led me onto a cross street. I walked briskly down that and just before I reached the corner, I came to an abrupt stop, put a cigarette between my lips and turned deliberately around. There was a man and a woman on the other side of the street, nobody else. I was certain I'd thrown Kane's man off my trail.

I took a cab downtown now, completely relaxed and just a little proud of myself. So I was a sap, according to Kane. If that happened to be true, his boys were in a still lower category.

Kane's address turned out to be a nice apartment house just off lower Fifth Avenue. There was no doorman, but, in passing, I noticed that the lobby was neat and cheerfully lighted. The rent here would be high. Too high for a fastliving cop no matter what his rank. If I had any luck at all, Kane's desire for good things was going to help defeat him.

The elevator was self-service and the row of lobby mail boxes gave me the number of Kane's apartment. I rode to the fifth floor, located 5C with no trouble at all and I took a good long listen at the door. I heard nothing at all and if Kane was in there, awake, I'd have heard his voice easily. It was the kind that carried.

Anyway, the situation called for risks so I pressed the buzzer and waited. Nothing happened. I buzzed again just to be sure, but I was already studying the lock and it wasn't an especially difficult one. I took a good look at the door frame too and that appeared to be even easier. I brought out my wallet, removed the thick cellophane window of the section where I carried my identification papers and shoved the strip of pliable substance between the door and the door frame until I could feel the lock tongue.

I wound my handkerchief around my fist, worried the cellophane strip further along the tongue and then I gave it a sharp twist. At the same time, I gave the door a solid bang with my muffled fist. The door sprang open. I laughed. So this was the apartment of Captain Kane, of the Burglary and Robbery Detail, who preached that a door should never be just slammed shut but double locked with a key.

I went through the place just to make sure he wasn't sleeping. It was a four-room affair and nobody was in it. I took a careful look around now. Just as Mona's research had indicated, Kane might spend plenty on himself so he could travel around with classy broads, but he spent damned little on his home. The bedroom furniture was cheap maple. The dining room set was nothing his grandmother had received from her mother. Rugs were thin and worn, the living room furniture was Grand Rapids modern and looked lumpy and uncomfortable, and in the kitchen I found what must have been the first electric ice box. Lucky Mrs. Kane with such a lovely home!

But the place was neat. Kane's wife must have had a lot of time on her hands and used it to keep the apartment up. I didn't see a speck of dust anywhere, but on a small kidneyshaped desk, which was about the most attractive piece of furniture in the living room, I spotted a piece of letter paper half filled with writing. Apparently Mrs. Kane had been busy composing this letter and had left it abruptly because the last sentence wasn't even finished.

I read the letter, what there was of it. Mrs. Kane's handwriting was the careful, perfectly formed script of a school teacher or a bookkeeper. The letter was addressed to Dearest Ellen:

It's nine o'clock already and not a word from Jack. It seems lately he doesn't even bother to phone when he's going to be late. It's always police work. Crime won't wait. I've heard it again and again until it drives me crazy. Sometimes I wonder if it is all police work. We're in debt again—deeply this time—and Jack refuses to worry about it. He draws a good week's pay, but I see so little of it. All I do is get up in the morning, give him breakfast and off he goes. Sometimes he's gone for eighteen or twenty hours. I used to worry that he'd get hurt. Lately, I worry that he won't. Ellen, I may not be able to stand this much longer and if it gets the best of me, I'll try to scrape together the price of the bus fare and come visit you and the children for a while. There's nothing to do here. Just sit and read. We can't even afford a TV set. I've taken to going out to a bar and grill just around the corner. I sit there for hours just looking at people and wishing someone would speak to me. Don't worry about me. I only drink a little beer. But all this scares me. Sometimes I think I could cheerfully kill him ....

I put the letter down and knew I had my answer. A lonely woman, frustrated, writing of murder—even though she didn't mean it—was absolutely ripe for the taking. I didn't bother to search the apartment because I had all I required now.

On the street, I hurried to the nearest corner. I saw no sign of a bar and grill, but I knew there had to be one. I found it around the other corner—a nice place catering to a respectable crowd and not very busy at this hour. I went in and ordered beer at the bar. While I drank it, I turned around and looked the patrons over. A woman alone stands out in a place of this kind, but this woman—and I hoped she was the one I was looking for—would have stood out anywhere.

She was sitting in one of the booths facing me. She was tawny-haired, and even at this distance I could see that she had striking amber eyes. She didn't wear much makeup and she was one of the few women I've ever seen who could wear a peasant blouse and still look attractive.

She struck me as being feline. The sort of woman who'd move quickly and might scratch while she purred contentment. She may have written Ellen that she drank beer, but she wasn't doing that tonight. There were two empty shot glasses in front of her and a third about half full. However, she seemed perfectly sober.

I downed the rest of the beer and then walked deliberately over to her booth. I was banking on the hope that boredom and loneliness might get the better of what usually was good judgement. I came to a stop at the booth and took off my hat.

I said, "Excuse me, miss. I'm extremely lonesome, I don't like drinking alone and I wonder if you'd let me sit down and talk to you. I expect nothing, want nothing except a few minutes of company."

She seemed amused and interested. "Well, that's a new method, at least. Why did you pick on me?"

"For two reasons." I gave her my best smile. "You're very attractive and—you seemed about as lonely as I feel."

"Sit down," she said. "I'd like to talk to you, but—" And she gave me a charming little smile—"I must tell you I'm married, I love my husband—and he happens to be a police captain."

I slid onto the seat across from her and signaled a waiter. She was drinking Scotch straight. I ordered Scotch for me and a fresh one for her.

"So your husband is a policeman," I said. "That's very interesting. I'm in the same line of work."

Her eyebrows shot up. "Really?"

"I'm a private investigator. My name is Richard Owen."

She put her hand across the table and we shook very solemnly. Then we both laughed and the atmosphere cleared. I gave her a story about as real as the name I'd given her. She listened intently and I could see what a little company meant to her. I tried not to stare at her, but it was hard. She was made to be looked at and admired.

She had one more Scotch and stopped cold, which I liked, too. Sometimes Mona drank too much, and, while her taste ran to champagne, she could get just as tight on that as she could on Scotch. Mrs. Kane knew exactly when to call it a day.

I found out her first name was Sheila, which I liked, too, and before the evening was over, I was using it when I talked to her.

But she did most of the talking; being the wife of a cop who was seldom at home wasn't any picnic.

"He keeps no regular hours, just works as long as he can stand it, and when he comes home he tumbles into bed exhausted. I wish he'd chosen some other profession. Like yours—with office hours. Or at least you can quit for the day when you want to. Jack never knows when to quit. If he were killed tomorrow, my life wouldn't seem any different."

"That's too bad," I said. "Especially since you like the guy. He ought to ease up. Even the police department doesn't expect its men to work like that."

"Well, he does and I don't think they could stop him. When we were first married and he was a street sergeant, we had fun, were together as often as he could manage it. He took an interest in everything around the house. Then they put him in the detective bureau and things changed."

"Doesn't he realize what he's doing to you?" I asked.

"I'm afraid not. He has his sights set on an inspector's badge and it would take an awful lot to stop him from getting it. All of his promotions came from hard work, and he's working all the harder to get his next jump in rank."

"Well," I said, "maybe he'll get it soon and then slow down."

She laughed and shook her head. "Not Jack. There are grades above an inspector. He won't stop until he's chief, and then I expect he'll be restless and unhappy because there's nowhere else to go."

I called the waiter over and paid for the drinks.

She seemed sorry to have the evening end, and as if she were afraid she'd bored me, said, "I'm sorry I talked so much. Next time, you'll pick someone without a grudge against life."

I chuckled, feeling very good. "I'd pick you again over anyone, Sheila. I think all this chatter did you a lot of good. Can I take you home?"

"No, I'd rather you didn't. People talk and Jack—well—I'm afraid not."

"All right," I said. "But if you feel the urge to talk some more, I'll drop in here occasionally. And please understand, I'm no more on the make than you are."

"I know." She gave me her hand again and I helped her out from behind the table. I had a better look at her then. She was built exactly as I knew she would be, which was just about perfect. This woman was loaded down with sex and as frustrated as any female I'd met in a long time. With the right kind of treatment I had an idea I might be able to make time with her, and it was an appealing thought. If I could hurt Kane through her, that was okay with me.

We parted at the corner and I watched her walk briskly toward her apartment house. Her walk made me want to follow her, but I didn't. If she went cold on me, she'd never warm up again, so I turned reluctantly away and went back in the direction of my hotel, forty-odd blocks uptown.

I knew I wasn't being followed now, and this was my best opportunity to get established as Richard Owen. I hailed a cab and had the driver take me to that smaller hotel on the street behind mine. I ducked across the sidewalk pretty fast. In a matter of minutes I became a guest, paying a week's rent in advance, and I promised to have my baggage delivered. I went up to my room, found it pleasant enough and stayed there about an hour. I wondered how Kane's boys felt, trying to locate me. I hoped they all had bunions.

I thought about Sheila, too. She had a quality that most women I had known lacked. Just what it was I didn't know, but the fact that she made me feel restrained and thoughtful was odd enough in itself. Anyway, the whole situation seemed so impossibly crazy I refused even to consider taking her away from Kane. Somehow I didn't think that form of revenge would hurt him half as much as it would her.

I thought about a lot of things, up until just after midnight, but Sheila predominated everything. And yet, before I left the room, I knew there'd be no change in my plans. She was Captain Kane's wife and I intended to use her. When it was all over, I'd know absolutely just how much Kane was in love with her.

I went around to my own hotel, strolled in and chatted with the desk clerk a couple of minutes. One of Kane's boys was parked in the lobby and the way he looked at me, when he was sure I didn't know it, indicated that I'd made no friend of him.

CHAPTER SIX

NEXT MORNING WHEN I walked into my office, Mona told me Marty Carroll had phoned and wanted me to call back. He was the fence who'd refused to buy any more of my gems.

"Good," I said. "Maybe he's changed his mind."

"Mike—I thought you might show up again last night. I waited until very late. ..."

I hung up my hat and scanned the mail while I said, "I told you I was going to see about Kane's wife. Well, I did."

"You managed to meet her?"

I looked up with a grin. "Sure—she's quite a doll."

Mona was holding a stenographer's book in her hand and she suddenly slammed it on the desk top. "Mike, you're out of your mind. She's a cop's wife. What's Kane going to do when he finds out?"

"Nothing. Not one God-damned thing, baby, because his wife is going to help me pull a job and be as guilty as I. I don't think Kane will let her take the rap along with me, and if he doesn't—he's cooked from then on."

"How do you know she'll help you? Mike, be reasonable."

I said, "Sheila Kane is lonely, sore at her husband, craving company and a few kind words. Kane doesn't stay home at all. He chases, as you learned, but Sheila doesn't know that. We're pretty good friends already and by the time I'm set to take that Brindley necklace, she'll be glad to give me a hand. Without knowing exactly what it's all about, of course."

Mona chewed off some of the rouge on her lower lip. "I'm not saying you can't get away with it, Mike. But the risk isn't worth it." Her black eyes got chillier and narrower. "Unless you're falling for Sheila Kane."

I didn't want to talk about it. Mona irritated me this morning. I said, "Let's get some work done. After all, we run a business—or what's left of it. Did Marty tell you when I should phone him back?"

"No. Any time, I suppose."

I looked up Marty's number, dialed it and he answered right away.

"Mike, I'm glad I reached you. Listen, I was a fool to turn you away. An old, crazy fool. You're one of my best clients, and if you have anything for me, bring it down."

"I'll see you this afternoon, around three," I said. "You'll need about twenty grand to do business with me, Marty."

"I'll have it ready—and maybe I'll warm your ears a bit, too. I don't like the way things are going, Mike, and if anybody can stop them, you can."

I wondered what he meant. Marty wasn't one to indulge in fantasies. If he said he knew something he didn't like, that was exactly how it would be. I was half tempted to drop everything and go see him right away. I didn't though. One of my oldest customers came in to tell me he wanted to clear up his account and we weren't going to do any more business together. I had Mona type out the account, accepted his check and I didn't even bother to try and find out what made him drop me that way. I knew.

I walked out at two-fifteen, though it required not more than twenty minutes to reach Marty's place. I needed time to throw Kane's shadows off my trail and the easiest way was by the route I'd already picked out for myself. I took a cab to my hotel, paid the driver before he stopped and was out of the taxi and through the lobby before that plain black sedan which had stuck behind us even had a chance to double park.

I got off the elevator at my floor, ran to the stairway and went down again. I passed through the porter's room without being seen, crossed the court and went over the fence. On the next street I hailed a cab and had myself driven to within three blocks of Marty's place. Then I walked briskly, doubled back a couple of times and made certain I'd thrown off the watchdogs.

Then I opened the door of Marty's shop and walked in. There was a stillness I didn't like.

"Marty!" I called out.

There was no answer. I went around behind his counter, sure something was wrong. This was a jewelry store, and no owner in his right mind would go off and leave the door unlocked.

I went into Marty's little workshop. A fluorescent light was on over the worktable. A wedding ring lay on a piece of dark velvet. I picked it up. Marty had been engraving the ring, but only one set of initials had been completed.

There was a storeroom further back, and I went there next. When I pushed open the door, I knew what had happened before I even turned on the light. There was an odor in that back room. One I hadn't smelled since Iwo and Okinawa. Blood has an odor all its own. I lit a match. Marty lay on his back, his head in a pool of his own blood. The match burned my fingers before I dropped it.

I turned on the light, kicked the door shut and knelt beside him. His shirt had been almost ripped off and his undershirt torn to shreds. Bruises covered every inch of his torso. They'd been made by a combination of punches and kicks. There were blue marks around his throat and his right ear was almost torn off. All this hadn't been done in seconds; someone had methodically beaten him to death.

I didn't touch him. I just got to my feet and stood there. Marty may have been a crook, but he'd harmed no one physically, and he was an old man, incapable of much resistance. I left the back room, wiping off the doorknob and the light switch. I wiped everything else I might have touched and went to the safe in the front of the store. It was closed and locked. Burglary hadn't been the motive for that killing.

It occurred to me that someone might have known I had a date with Marty, so this was no place for me. I got out of there fast, but first making certain that there was nobody to notice me. I walked north, entered a bar and had a double rye. I took it to a corner table, sat down and swilled it like a lush. Then I yelled for more.

Three double ryes later I wasn't feeling any better. I wanted to curse and I wanted to cry. Poor old Marty.

Why had he been murdered and in that horrible way? It must have been plain torture, with a purpose—and could that purpose also concern me? Marty had wanted to tell me something. He hadn't believed it so important that it wouldn't wait until I arrived, but nevertheless I thought I'd detected a note of urgency in his voice when we talked over the phone.

It seemed somehow shameful to have left him like that— undignified, half naked, dead. He'd been such a fussy little old man when he was alive. I was half tempted to go back, make him tidy and decent, but that was insane. I walked to the nearest subway station, rode uptown and headed for my office building. Mona was gone and the office locked up when I got there. I let myself in, wishing I'd brought along a bottle, but smoked cigarettes instead until I couldn't taste them any longer.

Murder placed a new slant on things. At least it did until I began using my head. What did that killing have to do with me? Nothing, of course. I'd just been the man who'd found the body. Marty and I had never been close; we shared no secrets. I didn't even know one other of his customers nor where he sold the gems I brought to him.

I had to forget Marty and what I saw at his shop. It was none of my business. It didn't matter one bit—but I drank myself into a mild alcoholic fog at dinner. I had to walk twenty blocks to sober up, and the only happiness I got out of it was the knowledge that Kane's boys were getting sore feet, too.

When I returned to my hotel, I had an idea my shadows would nestle down, too, with the hope of staying there for a while. I was in no hurry, so I changed into fresh clothes before I went out the back way, over the fence and showed myself briefly at the little hotel where I was known as Richard Owen.

By nine I sauntered into the same bar and grill around the corner from Kane's place and felt genuine disappointment when I didn't see Sheila anywhere about. I went to the same booth we'd shared the night before, hoping she would come. I'd been so damned certain of her last night, and yet I had no real reason to be.

Half an hour went by. I began seeing Marty Carroll again, all bloody and beaten. I knew that by now the cop on the beat would have found the door unlocked and would have discovered Marty.

Then Sheila came into the place and Marty's grisly image faded from my mind. I got up quickly and reached out a hand as she approached. I wanted to take her in my arms. Instead, I helped her get seated, ordered drinks and we silently toasted one another. I said, "Husband off chasing crooks again?"

She nodded glumly. "He came home way after midnight, slept until noon and then went right out. He didn't even touch breakfast."

"The guy is nuts."

She shook her head and smiled wanly. "No—but he has two wives—a badge and me."

"How much longer are you going to put up with it?"

"I don't know. Forever, I suppose. While he was sleeping this morning, a bill collector came and put up an awful fuss. I told Jack about it when he woke up, and he laughed and said no bill collector ever worried him."

I didn't understand this, and I said so. "If your husband is police brass—and captains are—he can't afford to get into financial trouble. It isn't normal for a man in his position not to give a damn."

"Well, he doesn't. He leaves all the worrying to me. Dick, I don't want to talk about him tonight."

I swallowed the last of my drink. "Okay, I'll provide the entertainment. You're not to ask any questions or make any objections. We're going places, beginning right now."

I took her to Henri's, an out of the way but lush little place where the food was the finest, drinks the best, and a small dance band provided some of the nicest music in New York. We ate and then we danced. The bill was high, but so were my sights. Sheila made the place seem plusher, the food better and the music dreamier. When we left the evening seemed as young as a kitten.

After Henri's we took in another place, a night club this time. The floor show wasn't bad. I don't think either of us saw much of it because we were too busy looking at one another. She'd warmed up some, and when the dancing began I pulled her close, as if I'd been dancing with her all of my life. Once I brushed my lips against her cheek and felt her stiffen, which stopped me.

It was one-thirty when I finally took her home. The lobby of her apartment house was empty and silent. We went over to one of the darker corners and I drew her to me. She was willing enough but scared, too. She kept looking toward the entrance, and I knew what worried her. Kane worried me, too.

I knew she wanted to go up to her apartment. I kissed her just once, not long or hard, and let go of her while I still had the will power to do it. She touched my cheek tenderly, turned and hurried to the elevator. I waited until the car started up and then I walked out.

I kept on walking for about half an hour. There was so much on my mind I couldn't sort it out, and the picture of Marty Carroll kept coming back. I was worried about that murder, unsure of myself about Sheila and sore at Kane. I put Kane and Marty out of my mind and concentrated on Sheila and my original plan to make a sucker out of her. Should I drop the whole thing? What did she mean to me, anyway? She was beautiful—wonderful—but I had doubts that I'd ever really make the grade with her. So what could I gain? And—she was Captain Kane's wife. Through her, I might be able to stop that slob in his tracks and keep him off my back indefinitely. Maybe he didn't care much about Sheila, but a detective captain on the Robbery Squad who lets his wife help a jewel thief put over a caper simply isn't long for a policeman's world. Only through Sheila could I get at him. I made up my mind nothing was going to stop me.

And while I fashioned that determination, I could feel her in my arms again—feel her lips against mine, her body close to me. I yelled for a taxi and gave the driver Mona's address.

She was getting ready for bed and had thrown a robe over her nightie before she let me in. I went over to her little bar and dumped about four shots of whisky into a glass, carried it to a chair and sat down heavily.

Mona watched me. "Mike, what's the matter?" she asked.

"Everything," I said. "But mostly Marty Carroll."

"What about him?"

I told her and added the details. "Somebody literally beat him to death. Punched and kicked him until he couldn't take any more and just died."

Mona sat down abruptly, her face a dead white. "Mike—who did it?"

"How in hell do I know? I got out of there as fast as I could."

She tucked her legs under her on the divan. "I've had a feeling, Mike. That's why I've been getting scared. Do you think Kane could have...?"

"Bumped Marty? For Christ's sake, why? Kane knew he was a fence and knew I did business with him. There was always a chance Kane could reach me through Marty, so why kill him? No—it's something else."

"And haven't you the vaguest idea?"

"Only some foggy notions. Maybe some of this pressure brought to bear on me wasn't exerted by Kane. Maybe there's somebody in the same line as we are who doesn't want our kind of competition. When I talked to Marty on the phone, he sounded sore about something. But Ernie Haver told me it was Kane putting on the heat."

"Haver could have lied," Mona said.

I nodded, for the same idea had occurred to me.

Mona moved her legs to the floor. "Come over and sit by me, darling. I've never seen you so worried."

The invitation was one I hadn't been seeking at the moment, but I accepted it eagerly enough. With my arms around her, gently touching the swell of her breast, I concluded that I was a damn fool. I didn't have to sneak into dark corners to get Mona, nor wonder if she'd repulse my advances. I tilted Mona's head back and kissed her as warmly as I would have kissed Sheila right then.

Mona exhaled sharply when I let go of her. "Brother," she said, "you really mean it tonight. How come?"

"Stop asking silly questions." I pulled the robe back from her shoulders. Her nightie was sheer, and the warmth of her came through as if she were naked.

"Mike," she held the flat of one hand against my chest, keeping me off for a moment, "did you see Sheila Kane tonight?"

"Yes, I talked to her."

"And you didn't get far, did you? That's why you came here. Damn you, Mike, you let another girl get you all excited and then come to me...."

I put my hand over her mouth and shushed her. "I saw Sheila because I'm setting her up. I'm going to pull that Brindley pearl necklace job, and Sheila's going to help me. When it's over, she'll be a crook, too, and if Kane presses me too hard, he'll find about it. He'll discover that if he sends me up, his beautiful wife goes right along."

She was biting at the palm of my hand. I let her go, but while the explanation seemed to satisfy her to a certain extent, she was still shooting sparks.

"If I could only believe that," she said.

I pushed her away from me. "I told you facts. If you can't believe them, what's the use in my staying here?"

"No, Mike," she cried. She grabbed my arm, yanked me toward her, threw both arms about my neck and pulled me down. She was more than ready for my kiss this time.

But I kept seeing Sheila, thinking she was in my arms, wishing she were.

Mona got up long enough to turn off all the lights. Even the darkness didn't help. Sheila came shining right through. I tried to concentrate. It was no use. It was Sheila in my arms, Sheila I kissed, Sheila's hot breath against my chest. I felt like yelling my head off in exasperation.

When I got home and tumbled into bed, I knew one thing. I had to have Sheila. Afterwards, it wouldn't matter. I could go through with my plans and use her for a sap, but first she had to be all mine. And I knew I wouldn't wait very long.

CHAPTER SEVEN

I COULDN'T CONCENTRATE the next day. There wasn't much business anyway, and I didn't resent the fact. I fiddled around with that little necklace-snipping device, using Mona as a model, until I was really proficient in the use of the thing.

Mona seemed exceptionally happy, and I guessed that she was satisfied that my interest in Sheila was purely material. We went over my plans for the Brindley job. Mona was good at estimating the chances, weighing facts and generally helping me get the whole thing set up.

Around two in the afternoon Ernie Haver walked in. He didn't seem to remember the pushing around I'd given him a couple of days before. But Ernie just then was a badly worried young man.

He said, "Mike, what do you think about Marty Carroll's murder?"

"He's dead. Some stinker killed him and that's all there is to it."

"But why?"

"That's a matter for the police, not us, Ernie. Remember that Marty was no saint. Any fence makes enemies. Marty was okay to me, probably to you as well, but how do we know how he treated others? Some goon may have walked in with a doodad he wanted to sell and Marty may have tried to gyp him a little. There could be a hundred reasons."

Ernie wrinkled his nose. "You're not kidding me any. Besides, there's something you don't know. Marty called me up the day he was killed. I'd never heard him sound so sore. He asked me if there'd been any pressure put on me. I told him Kane's men had been around—mostly about you, Mike. Marty said he knew all about that, but had anybody been to see me since then. Well, nobody had and I told him so."

I pursed my lips and looked down my nose. "Marty called me too, Ernie. He said almost the same thing to me. I didn't get it then and I don't now."

Ernie sighed. "I hoped he might have been more explicit with you. Listen, do you think Kane had anything to do with it?"

"That's funny, Ernie, because Mona had the same idea. I don't think so. Kane is after me and he wouldn't stop at much to land me, but how would the murder of Marty help him? It just doesn't tie in."

Ernie stood up and adjusted his hat. He cut quite a figure. That guy could have fingered Queen Elizabeth's crown and gotten away with it.

"I give up," he said. "But just the same, I'm taking a vacation. I'm not very happy about all this. Anyway, pretty soon all the rocks will travel south and I'd be following them. Good luck, Mike. I don't blame you for slapping me around the other night. I'm forgetting it, and if I run into something big, I'll give you a buzz."

"Do that," I said. "And stop worrying about what happened to Marty."

I walked with Ernie to the door. I was more worried than I wanted him or anyone else to know. The fact that Marty had phoned Ernie too, and wanted to know if Ernie had been approached meant something. And he was right to wonder what. I would have envied Ernie going away like that if it hadn't been for Sheila.

Mona and I went back to practicing with the gimmick. My freedom could depend on the use of it, and I wanted no slips.

The closer it got to the dinner hour, the more nervous I became. I was going to see Sheila, and something would happen.

I doubted I could go through another evening without more definite physical contact with her. How she'd take that I didn't know—didn't much care. The one thing I felt sure of was the fact that she'd come to that little bar and grill.

And she not only came but beat me there by fifteen minutes. She held out both hands to me, and we didn't stay there very long—just for a couple of drinks. Then I suggested more dancing. Even if I hadn't found Sheila stimulating to be with, she would have excited me that night. It was like taking a beautiful kid out on her first big date. Her eyes were radiant as if everything she saw was new. The good food, the courteous waiter, the smooth band—

However, as I knew it was bound to come, she began asking questions about me. I was a vague character named Dick Owen, a private eye who never talked about his work or himself, and she wanted to know.

"I work out of my hotel room," I explained. "A private detective doesn't need an office unless he's searching for clients. Mine are all under contract to me. I specialize in jewelry cases. For insurance companies, mostly. I attend high-hat affairs and guard insured gems. If they're lifted, I try to track them down."

"It's odd you haven't run across my husband," she said. "He's in exactly the same line."

"Maybe I've seen him, possibly even talked to him without knowing who he was by name. I don't work with the police because sometimes my methods are, shall we say, a trifle unorthodox. You see, I want stolen gems back and I don't care much how I get them." Then I invented a few episodes to make it all sound authentic.

She was drinking frozen daiquiris all the while and she finished her third one before she spoke again. There was a wistful look in her eyes.

"I wish I could do something like that, Dick. Something exciting. I go crazy all by myself all day and most of the night."

There was the opening—the situation I'd planned to create deliberately was cropping up all by itself.

"Sheila, would you like to help me out some night?"

"How, Dick?"

"There's a society ball in a few days. The Fairweathers are giving it. A lot of insured gems will be worn, and I'm ordered to be on the job. Up to now I've always worked solo, but this job is too big. I could use an assistant."

She smiled and shook her head. "I wouldn't know a jewel thief if I ran head on into one, Dick."

"But you can spot a woman wearing a fortune in jewels. You could watch them to notice if any rocks you spotted seemed to be suddenly missing."

"Yes," she admitted doubtfully, "I could do that." Then she shook her head vigorously. "Jack will know about that affair and probably go there, too. If he found me there—I honestly don't know what would happen."

I still pressed my point, not being able to afford losing her now. "All right. There's another angle. At a party like this, there are always a lot of outside servants hired for the occasion. They have to be watched, too. You could stay in the kitchen and keep an eye on them. That's very important."

"Yes." She rested her chin in the palm of her hand. "I'd be doing something. It would take the edge off for a little while, at least. If Jack showed up, you could warn me."

"Of course."

"Then I'll do it. If you want me to, I'll be there, but I wish I knew more about what I was supposed to do."

I saw another chance. This was my lucky night. "Sheila, I can show you pictures of known jewel thieves. If you'd come to my hotel…."

She smiled a little. "Do you think that's very wise, Dick?"

I was trying not to show how I felt. "Of course I can bring them with me next time we meet…."

She laughed. "Dick, don't be silly. I'll go to your hotel with you. After all, I'm sort of an employee now."

I fed her two more drinks before I paid the check. We took a cab to my hotel. It was risky because, although I'd thrown off Kane's boys, some of them were bound to be watching my own hotel just around the corner. However, we got in without being observed. In this hotel, nobody cared much who went up or down in the elevators. Maybe the operator was interested, but that was all. I unlocked the door and Sheila preceded me into the room.

I closed the door. "It's not much of a place," I said apologetically.

"Why, I think it's nice, Dick."

"You know, of course, that there is no rogue's gallery of jewel thieves here."

She looked straight at me. "Yes, darling, I know."

I grabbed her hungrily, and, as I kissed her, she clung to me. There was no pretense about Sheila. In her was a long stored-up hunger for love and affection, things her damned fool husband had given up for his work and for chasing around with dames who couldn't compare to Sheila even remotely. I wouldn't have felt that I was doing Jack Kane a dirty trick, even if I had liked him. Besides, after tonight Sheila would be bound to me more firmly than ever.

I held her at arm's length for a moment. "You can still walk out, baby."

"Do you want me to, Dick?"

"God, no!" I exclaimed.

"Most men wouldn't have waited this long. Dick, I'm no wanton woman. I don't give myself to anyone who comes along. For me, this is the first time. But I know that Jack cheats on me. He thinks I'm fooled completely, but I know. A wife usually does. And I've been so damned lonesome for so long."

"If you stay..." I said.

"I'm not a child, darling. I grew up long ago."

She stepped back suddenly and took off the little bolero jacket she was wearing. She threw it onto a chair, zipped the dress open, lifted it by the hem and pulled it over her head. I drew a sharp breath and took her in a rough embrace. Something deep inside of me said I was going too far. This was a time to stop, to turn and run. A man in my position couldn't afford complications, and Sheila was a giant-sized complication. My thoughts weren't. I shoved them to one side.

"I think I'm in love with you, Dick," she whispered.

I knew she felt the shudder which went through me. I was playing a hell of a game with her. Every time she uttered that phony name she knew me by, it was like telling a lie.

There were too many lights in the room, but they showed up the whiteness of her, the wonder of her. She was here now for me to have and to know. She waited for my move, anticipated it and clung to me fiercely. My mind was suddenly clear, containing only the desire for her. All else vanished, left me feeling at ease for the first time in days. The softness of her body and the hardness of her muscles were against me, straining, asking, imploring. We did no more talking.

We stood there, near the open window, feeling the cool, late summer breeze filtering through. "I can't let you go after this," I said.

"I know, darling. I know just how you feel because it's the way I feel. Dick, I don't know what we're going to do about this, and right now I don't care. I don't even want to talk about it. Do you?"

Then we turned back and soon a gale could have stormed in through the window and we'd not have noticed it. I was lost in the wonder of the simple and genuine love she had for me. She whispered it over and over when she regained her breath. Then we both became quiet . . . .

I turned a bit and blinked. Somebody had switched on the damn lights. I remembered Sheila and sat upright. Sunlight was streaming in through the window. I said, "Sheila!" somewhat sharply. There was no answer. I got up quickly and then laughed to myself. Where could anyone hide in one room? I could still smell her perfume and vividly recall how she'd felt in my arms. It was nine o'clock in the morning and I grinned somewhat fool-ishly at myself in the mirror. Of course she'd slipped out while I was asleep. She was quite a girl.

I stepped under the shower and started singing in full voice, trying to remember the last time I'd done that. I was still sing-ing—if that's what you'd call it—while I dried off, shaved and then dressed. It didn't hit me until I put on my tie, standing real close to the mirror. Then I nearly garoted myself with my own necktie. I was in love!

I backed up to the chair, sat down heavily and stuck a ciga-rette between my lips. I forgot to light it. Sheila was married to a man who was more dangerous to me than anyone else on earth. Kane would never let her go, least of all to a guy like me. If a man he'd tagged as a crook got her, it would drive him nuts. And yet it would have to happen. I knew I couldn't do without her.

Then a second problem hit me. How could I use her in this lousy racket when I thought of her as I did? A man doesn't risk the liberty and happiness of a girl he's in love with, and all of a sudden I realized I was no different than anyone else. Instead of hurting Sheila, I wanted to protect her.

But I wanted the Brindley pearls, too. I knew exactly where I could get rid of them at a good price and in a hurry. Being caught between two desires like that was a novel experience to me. I hated the sensation because I'd always prided myself on the fact that when I made up my mind to pull a job, there'd be nothing to stop me.

I walked the floor, swearing softly, until I realized there was nothing to prevent me from having both the pearls and Sheila. I'd talk Mona into the job. That would be better all around because Mona had expert experience behind her. If she was a bit nervous now, she'd lose all that by the time the job was to be pulled. I'd make her.

This decided upon, I walked out of the hotel and suddenly remembered Kane's boys. I decided to let them work out their own problems and went directly to the office. Mona wasn't in yet, and I spent about an hour going over my assets. I wondered if Sheila would consider simply leaving Kane and going away with me. If I added the Brindley profits to what I already had, we could live well for years. I had to put that job over.

Mona breezed in about eleven. We kept beautiful office hours. Not that it mattered any more. My business was in a slump that went all the way down to zero. The only good feature about it was the fact that I could convert what stock I had in a matter of hours.

Mona shed her jacket and hat, came over and kissed me on the back of the neck, then started running her fingers through my hair. "I sort of expected you last night, Mike," she said. "The way you acted the night before I was pretty sure...."

"I was out with Sheila," I said.

She straightened up and gave me a significant look. Then she went around to the other side of the desk, put her hands flat on it and leaned over to stick her face close to mine.

"You're a good-looking guy, Mike. You've got baby blue eyes that drive women crazy, your hair curls a little and it's a nice shade of brown. Your personality is plus and you make love like no one I ever met."

"What's all the build-up for?"

"Is that Sheila Kane falling for you?"

"I don't know, kid."

Her eyes flashed signals I should have recognized. "Maybe you're falling for her, Mike."

I leaned back in my chair. "Look, Mona, she's a nice kid. Too damned nice to get mixed up in this racket. Besides, I don't feel that I can trust her."

"You thought she was indispensable the last time we talked about it."

"I know, but things have changed."

"Then the Brindley job is off?"

"I didn't say that. I want you to help me."

She bit her lip, straightened up and studied me for a moment. "You're in love with her, aren't you, Mike? Own up. You can tell me."

"I like her too much to make a sucker out of her," I said curtly. "Let it go at that."

"The hell we will," Mona flared. "So she's out and I'm in. If I get tossed in the can—that's okay. You don't give a damn about that. But I do."

"Oh, come on, Mona," I said uncomfortably.

"You're asking me to step aside and let Sheila take you over," she went right on to say. "That's bad enough, but now I'm to help you pull a job I considered too dangerous to begin with. Talk about suckers!"

"There'll be twenty-five grand in it for you, baby," I said.

"I've got all the money I need. Mike—tell me the truth. Have you fallen for this little bitch?"

I was in no mood to argue. I got to my feet.

"Okay, baby, you've got it right, and Sheila doesn't fit in with your four-letter word vocabulary."

She came around the corner of the desk and flew at me. The attack was so unexpected I didn't have a chance to get set. Her nails made two raw tracks down my cheeks, and she was set to claw me again. I gave her a shove that sent her reeling back. But whether Mona's blood was Spanish or Gypsy, it was hot as Old Faithful. She picked up an ash tray and hurled it. I got a face full of ashes, though the heavy glass missed my head by a couple of inches.

She picked up the base of a pen set and got ready to throw it, but I rushed her and twisted the thing out of her hand. She kicked my shins and my legs, did her best to use a knee on me, and all the while her free hand came at my face with those talons ready and eager. There was only one thing I could do.

I gave her another shove, letting go of her wrist at the same time. When she flew back, I wound one up and hammered it smack to her jaw. She had her mouth open to yell and the teeth came together with a snap. She landed against a chair, made a few wild grabs at it and slid to the floor in a heap.

I cursed her and went to the bathroom for a glass of water. I fed this to her until she opened her eyes. My arm was supporting her and as soon as she had the strength, she brushed it away and managed to get on her feet without my help. The fight was out of her—the active kind, at least—but she was hating me with her eyes.

"We're finished, Mike. You know that," she said.

"I'm sorry, baby. I apologize for punching you, but there was nothing else I could do."

"Forget the punch. I can—but not the double-cross you just handed me. I'm getting out, Mike."

I said, "I wish you wouldn't," but knew while I spoke that this was the best way all around. "You have more money coming, baby. I'll give it to you now if you still intend to walk out."

"I don't want your money and you're goddam right I'm walking out. That doesn't mean I've finished with you. I'll fight you every chance I get. I'll be as low as you've been and that's getting down pretty far. You'll be sorry about this, Mike. You'll wish Sheila had never been born."

I went around to the back of my desk and sat down. "So long, Mona," I said quietly. "Good luck."

She snatched up her hat and threw her jacket over her shoulders. "I'm not wishing you any luck except the kind that's all bad. You didn't know I could hate this way, did you, Mike? You haven't seen the half of it. And as for that Brindley necklace, you won't get it. That's going to be mine—if I have to kill you to stop you."

She stormed out, slamming the door hard. I heaved a great sigh and wished all this hadn't happened. Mona had been too close to me. But sooner or later she had to go.

I was half tempted to bundle up everything I owned, call Sheila and make her leave everything behind and go off with me at once. That was the wise and peaceful way. But Mona was going after the Brindley necklace too; that put it down as a definite challenge. My appetite for those pearls was now voracious.

CHAPTER EIGHT

L IFE DURING THE next week was lousy. Without Mona around the office it was too quiet, so I spent little time there. Nights I sat in that bar and grill waiting for Sheila. She didn't come for three nights, and when, on the fourth, she did show up, she could only stay for a moment or two.

"I knew you'd be worried, darling," she said. "But this week—of all weeks—Jack decided to take some time off. He doesn't stay home much, but he comes and goes. He only just left, but there's no telling when he'll be back, so I can't stay."

"We've got to do something about him, Sheila."

"I know. I've been trying to find the solution and I can't. Mike—I did something perhaps I shouldn't have ..."

I grabbed both her hands across the table. "You just called me Mike."

"That's what I was about to explain. You—fell asleep that night. That wonderful night, darling. I was going to lay out some fresh clothes for you so when you woke, you'd know you hadn't been dreaming. But there wasn't anything in the dresser drawers, nothing in the clothes closet. Then your wallet fell out of your pocket and I—I peeked."

"So now you know I was giving you a line," I said bitterly.

"Mike, do you think I care now? Though, of course, I'm curious. What are you—really?"

"A jeweler," I said. "A very high-hat jeweler. A lot of the stuff I told you was true. When I sell someone valuable merchandise, I try to protect it. There's been plenty of thievery going on lately and it doesn't do my business any good when a customer pays a hundred thousand for an item and has it swiped soon afterwards."

"Then this Fairweather affair is still on?"

"Yes," I said. I had to use her now; there was no way out of it.

"And we're both going?"

"If you still want to and that husband of yours doesn't stick his lousy nose into it."

Sheila looked down at the table for a moment. "I'm getting to the point where I don't care, Mike. I'm in love with you and that changes everything."

I wanted to take her in my arms but all I did was pat her hand.

"I'll be here every night. Come if and when you can."

"All right, Mike. And I'm going with you to that party no matter what. Now I'd better run."

She leaned across the table and pressed her cheek against mine before she went back to her apartment. I stayed in the joint another hour, sampling rye until I was unsteady on my feet and calling myself an idiot for giving way like that. If I kept it up, I'd be in fine shape to snatch that Brindley necklace.

The next day something happened which didn't improve the situation any, either. A smart artist at lifting jewelry that didn't belong to him was found in the river. He'd been dead when they threw him in, according to the newspaper items, and the medical examiner had stated he'd been savagely beaten to death.

Like Marty Carroll, this man had been no cheap punk. He dealt in only the best, timed his jobs well and had never been arrested even on suspicion. I'd known him and liked him, and the manner of his death gave me a mild case of nerves. Without seeing his corpse, I knew the same people had worked him over. Like Marty he had either refused to talk or had held something out.

Sheila came to the bar the night before the big job. Outside the joint I had a brand new car parked, and, after we downed a couple of drinks, I took her to it and let her admire six thousand dollars' worth of chromium and leather. Then we drove cross-town, hit the speedway and headed for the country.

It was one of those New York nights which are like a weather bonus: warm enough but not at all hot, with a three-quarter moon making everything glimmer with silver. Soon we left the skyscraper terrain, and pretty little houses began to flash by. For the first time in my life I thought living in one of those would be nice.

I finally located a likely looking side road, turned down it and bumped over ruts for a couple of miles until I found a turn-off. I stopped the car, put out the lights and reached for Sheila.

She tucked her head against my shoulder. "Mike," she said in a whisper, "I can't do without you again. I know that now—after these centuries since the last time we met. It's hit me so hard that I—I often think I'll kill Jack, just to get away."

I pushed her up in considerable alarm. "Don't say that! Don't even think it! Sheila, we couldn't be happy if you ..."

She put a finger against my lips and smiled. "Mike, you know I couldn't."

"That's better. I don't like your husband, but murder is low, and it's never a solution to any problem."

"If there were only some other way," she said dreamily.

I was thinking the same thing. An idea had hit me some time back. Not the kind I liked, but, while it would mean considerable sacrifice on my part, it also might work in my favor and Sheila's too. To explain it, I had to come perfectly clean with her. She might be shocked, but not as badly as if the news reached her through another source.

She wasn't in a listening mood at the moment. She had wedged herself in the far corner of the seat and had her arms stretched out for me.

I said, "Sheila, I want you very badly, but first there's some-thing I've got to tell you."

She moved over beside me. "Why, Mike, you sound so serious."

"I am. Now understand, if I wasn't crazy in love with you, I'd never say this, but I must. Our meeting in that bar and grill was no accident."

"Really?" She arched her eyebrows. "Explain yourself, darling."

"I was looking for something to pin on your husband. We've been enemies for a long time. That night I got into your apartment. I read the letter you had written to someone named Ellen ..."

"My aunt," she said. "Go on, Mike."

"That gave me an idea. I thought if I could make you, induce you to help me with a little scheme that is quite illegal to put it mildly, I'd implicate you so much Kane would be forced to forget my part in it."

She said, "You made those plans before you met me, Mike?"

"Yes. I carried them around after I met you, too, but not for long. I realized I couldn't possibly mix you up in this. You see, Sheila, I'm more than a jeweler ...."

She suddenly smiled. "You're one of the smartest jewel thieves in the business," she said.

I just sat there gaping.

"Mike, I'm a cop's wife. My husband is on a detail which fights you. I've heard him mention your name. He hates you like poison. Then—when I snooped into your wallet—well, I knew, that's all."

"And it didn't make any difference?"

"I'm in love with you, not with what you are. Though it'll be quite a change from being the wife of a cop to the sweetheart of a crook."

"You're wonderful!" I said. "And it was so damned hard to tell you ..."

"Don't underestimate a woman's love, Mike. But I'm warning you, I'll try to change you."

"I know. I hope you do because I'm sick of all this. Alone, I didn't care. The risks were an appealing part of the racket, but with you to think about I'd make a lousy thief."

"What about the Fairweather business then?"

I said, "That's where I intended to use you. By letting you think I was a private detective and that you were helping me, I'd have swiped a certain necklace, slipped it to you and told you to meet me somewhere else with it. Or maybe planted it on you without your knowing about it at all. In any event, you'd be implicated and your husband wouldn't have been able to act against me without taking sides against you also. It's all changed now."

"You're not going through with it?"

"No—not to get the necklace for myself. But I might use the same setup to throw your husband off balance."

Sheila asked me for a cigarette. I lit it and she blew a big mouthful of smoke out of the car window. "Mike, I didn't mean to tell you this, but one night about a week ago Jack came home half drunk, and reeking of perfume. When I called him on it, he sat there and boasted of the women he'd been out with. Then he knocked me down—because I began to cry. I don't care what happens to him. He's no good. Besides, he'd kill you if he thought you and I..."

"I hated him before," I said fervently, "but now I feel like committing murder too. Sheila, would he let you go if you asked him?"

"So I could go with you? Mike, he'd kill me too rather than do that."

"But suppose he was a busted cop? What would that do to him?"

"I think he'd go crazy."

"That's what I thought. Sheila, is it all right if I wreck him?"

"How else can we be together?" she asked. "After last week, I don't care what happens to him."

I said, "Okay, he's going to be so busy with trouble he'll want none with you. He'll start sliding down after this happens. He'll go so low you can divorce him. Leave that part to me. Is it a deal?"

She put her arm around my neck. "I wish you didn't talk so much, Mike. ..."

"But is everything all right with you? After what I've told you?"

"Everything is fine. Or will be when you realize you've got a woman in your arms who is in love with you."

"It will be too late to back out once we set the stage," I warned.

"Damn it, Mike, I know that. Don't disconcert me. To hell with Jack. There's just you and me here. Only the two of us."

"There are things you have to know," I said. "Details."

"Tell them to me afterwards. Mike, I swear ..."

She saw the grin on my face, smiled in return as I held out my arms for her and came to me again. Everything was much more gentle tonight. Our kisses were just as fierce, I suppose, but there was a difference too. The urgency was gone. We knew one another, trusted and respected one another. We were in love too—self-confessed lovers, sure of ourselves and all that we did.

Sheila was stroking my face now, murmuring softly, completely at ease. Her hair had fallen down over her forehead and she looked so damned pretty I just stared at her. She pushed my hair back and kissed me.

"Don't worry about me, Mike," she said. "I'm strong. I'm much stronger than you think. That's Jack's trouble. He doesn't understand me and he never will, but I think you do." "I doubt it, baby. Now the angle is this. We've got to deflate your husband to a point where he doesn't give a damn what happens to him. You helped to build him up and now I'm pushing him down again—way down. There'll be trouble, but it ought to come out fine in the end. I just want you to know it can also be dangerous."

"I can handle Jack," she said. "When you lose respect for a man, you learn how to handle him."

"I'm thinking of something else. Sheila, tell me the truth about this. Has your husband been talking about getting me?"

"Only in the sense that you're a law breaker and he's a policeman. I don't think he implied that he'd like to kill you."

I said, "A couple of friends of mine were murdered in the last two days. Crooks, like me, but decent guys in their own way. Besides, someone has been putting a lot of pressure on me. Customers have stopped coming, people I did business with refuse to see me any more. One of them was Marty Carroll, but all of a sudden he had a change of heart and decided to defy whatever pressure group had worked on him. I went to see him and I found him dead."

Sheila said, "Jack wasn't responsible for that, Mike. I won't believe it of him. Snide, cruel tricks—yes. A good old double-cross—that's in his makeup, but not murder."

"Just the same," I said, "two people are dead. Oh, well, maybe it has nothing to do with me. I've had the jitters lately anyway. Right now there's only one thing that means much—you and me. Anything else doesn't matter and anything we do to make sure we stay together is okay."

She was looking at me thoughtfully. "Mike, darling, you intended to steal this necklace all along, didn't you?"

I nodded. "Sure, but you changed my mind."

"If Jack refuses to let me go, if you can't break him, there is only one thing we can do. Go away together—and that costs money. I don't know how you're fixed, but these pearls should bring a good price..."

I grabbed her by both shoulders. "Are you asking me to swipe them? Is that what you want?"

She smiled. "Mike, I've always believed a woman should have enough faith in her man's profession to help him when she can."

I leaned back. "I'll be damned. All right—that's what we'll do, if things turn out well. If they don't—if your husband should be there—we'll let the necklace go and work him over. Either way we can't lose."

"Then I'm to be there and help you all I can."

"Exactly. Baby, you've restored a lot of self-confidence in me."

"Just promise me you'll be careful," she said.

"Bank on it. I have a damned good reason to keep my health now."

She seized my hands, held them tightly and leaned toward me. In the middle of our kiss her fire leaped out to rekindle mine. Then I no longer had any doubts. I knew things would turn out the way we wanted them to because they had to. Our whole future and happiness was at stake. With such a goal held out for us, we couldn't fail. She knew it and I knew it.

CHAPTER NINE

Getting Sheila installed in the kitchen was a cinch. There were so many outside servants around the Fairweather estate nobody could keep track of them. I picked her up near her apartment. She wore a tailored suit with a small corsage of flowers and she could have passed for anything at that party. Even one of the guests.

She didn't know anything about Kane's activities for the evening. He'd left in the middle of the morning without saying when he'd be back. But after I'd installed Sheila in the kitchen, I walked around the house and came through the big double doors into the reception hall, and I saw a couple of Kane's men posted there. Both of them all but came to attention when I entered. So far as they were concerned, I was the guest of honor at this show, and there'd be no necklace stolen tonight. My alternate plan still held, however.

I wondered what kind of treatment they'd been getting from Kane lately. For days now, I'd thrown them off my trail at will, and they hadn't tumbled to that rear exit yet nor the fact that I lived a double life and maintained another hotel room. The game was beginning to bore me, however, and I was glad it was almost over.

I knew many of the guests and most of them knew me. A few studiously avoided me, but not Mrs. Brindley. She was a plump, sincere widow of about fifty-two with enough dough to attract all sorts of younger men. She showed little interest in them. She was friendly, anything but domineering, and I thought she'd react exactly the way I wanted her to.

I stayed away from her for an hour or so, but I couldn't afford to wait too long. Kane might show up and if he stumbled into the kitchen and saw Sheila, there was going to be trouble. So I sought out Mrs. Brindley again.

"I refuse to wait any longer for a dance," I said with such charm I almost charmed myself. Then I reminded her that I'd always thought her a wonderful dancer.

"Why, thank you," she said. "You know, Mike, I can always relax with you and enjoy myself. I don't have to wonder if this is the first step in an ardent courtship meant to sweep me off my feet."

"And sweep a few millions into a gaping pocket," I added. "No, not me, Mrs. Brindley. When I take your money I'll have earned it." I put my arm around her and led her onto the floor. She really was a good dancer and I enjoyed myself. But I had to push things along a bit. For some reason I was getting scared.

I said, "Your pearls are as lovely as ever."

She let go of my hand, reached up and touched them. "I do that every time I think of them, Mike. I often wonder if it's worth the risk—wearing a fortune like this around my neck."

"You own them," I said. "You might as well wear them. I— Mrs. Brindley, has that clasp been giving you any trouble?"

"Clasp? Why, no."

"The pearls seem to sag a bit. Maybe the string has stretched. It could even be slipping out of the clasp. Would you like me to look at them?"

"Oh my—I should hate to lose them, Mike. Of course I want you to look at them. Where can we ...?"

I danced her toward one of the small rooms off this depot-like ballroom. We found it empty, walked in and I closed the door behind us. Then I stepped up to Mrs. Brindley and started removing the necklace. She couldn't see what I was doing and as the beads slipped off her neck, I grasped the clasp end and gave it a twist and a yank. Usually the kind of thread used in a necklace like this can't be easily broken, but I knew exactly how to do it. Most of the strands gave way. I walked around to face her, examining the necklace closely.

"I thought so," I said. "Look for yourself, Mrs. Brindley."

She saw her necklace and let out a mild cry of dismay. "Why, it's almost broken. They might have spilled all over the floor. Mike, I don't know how to thank you."

"No need to," I said. "If you recall, this necklace was in my shop not too long ago and I should have noticed this. I feel it's all my fault and I intend to rectify my carelessness."

"Oh, that isn't necessary at all," she said. "These things will happen."

I said, "Mrs. Brindley, I can restring this necklace in an hour. With your permission I'll take it to my shop right now, do the job and return it in time so you can be wearing it again at supper. I insist."

"Well," she said, "I would like to wear it, Mike."

"Good," I said. "Don't worry about a thing. Leave it to me."

I slipped the necklace into my pocket, showed her out of the room, and in a gesture that she thought was done in fun, I danced her across the ballroom before I let her go. Then I hurried toward the door.

There were two men behind me. Men in tuxedoes who should have been given instructions about how to wear them. Two more appeared from somewhere and beat me to the door. Another one went out for a moment and when he returned, a dour Captain Kane was behind him. Kane walked directly up to me. Normally his voice was no lullaby and when he was sore, it climbed a few extra degrees. He was sore now.

"Okay, Sloan," he said. "I've been waiting a long time for this. Hoist 'em."

"Now just a minute," I objected, backing away a step or two.

One of Kane's boys cuffed me along the back of the head and gave me a push that landed me in Kane's arms. He shoved me against the wall so hard there was an audible thump. Then he started searching me. It didn't take him long to find the necklace. He lifted it out of my pocket with a grunt of extreme satisfaction.

"Pretty, ain't it?" He held the pearls dangling in front of my eyes. "Take a good look, Sloan. You'll see this necklace just once more, when it's identified in court as the object you stole."

"Now see here, Kane," I said angrily. "You're accusing me of stealing this necklace in front of a lot of people. Persons who are, used to be, or could be customers of mine. If you must make such an accusation, you might be decent enough to do it in private."

"Private?" Kane howled. "Listen to him, boys. He's acting like a goddam duke or something. Go ahead, Sloan, explain why you've got Mrs. Brindley's necklace and no matter what you say, I won't believe you."

Kane hauled out a pair of handcuffs and slapped them on. I helped him by raising both hands and holding them poised to receive the circles of steel. I wanted those cuffs on me because there wasn't much more time. Through the shocked audience Mrs. Brindley was pushing her way toward me.

I said, "Is this an arrest, Captain?"

"Of course it's a pinch. One I've been aching to make for months."

"And the charge is theft of Mrs. Brindley's necklace?"

"Stop asking silly questions. Okay, Sloan, come on and I'll give you your first taste of a jail cell. I don't doubt you'll be bailed out in no time, only you're going into a cell first, no matter what."

He grabbed my elbow and shoved me toward the door. That was when Mrs. Brindley got in his way. Kane tipped his hat. A real gent.

"What's the meaning of this?" she demanded.

Kane gave a delighted chuckle. "Feel of your neck, Mrs. Brindley. Your pearls are gone. That's how we work. Show you the missing stuff before you realize it's gone."

"I know it's gone," she said angrily. "I gave that necklace to Mr. Sloan a few minutes ago because it needed repairing. Did you accuse him of stealing it?"

Kane's face went dead. Then he looked at me, and it came back into fiery life.

I said, "You made a little mistake, Captain Kane. It may be a very costly mistake. Take off these cuffs. I'm no criminal."

Kane turned to Mrs. Brindley. "What kind of a racket is this? He swiped that necklace and you know he did. He's been planning it for weeks."

Mrs. Brindley threw sparks. "I have done business with Mr. Sloan for several years. I respect him as an honest and capable man. This is not a racket, and I think I shall convince you of that very soon. I gave Mr. Sloan the necklace. It needs repairing. Would a thief offer to make such repairs? Especially when I know him so well? Take off those handcuffs, you imbecile. You … you … whoever you are."

I said, gently, "Mrs. Brindley, this is Captain Kane of the Police. He's suffering under the delusion that I'm some sort of thief. A mistake I'm planning to sue him for."

"He called me a racketeer," Mrs. Brindley fumed. "I'll sue him too. Will you remove those handcuffs?"

Kane fumbled for his keys and unlocked the cuffs, and I massaged my wrists as though they'd been wounded. Mrs. Brindley snatched the pearls out of Kane's hand and gave them to me. I dropped them into the same pocket.

I was enjoying myself. This couldn't have come off any better. Kane knew I'd planned it, and there wasn't a thing he could do. That's what I thought, but he suddenly grabbed me again, pushed me back against the wall and went through every pocket. I didn't know what I might have that he wanted. I thought the guy had simply gone off his rocker with embarrassment and chagrin. But the search was thorough, and he showed keen disappointment in not finding what he'd been after.

I brushed my tuxedo and looked very mortified. "Would you tell me what that was about, Captain? Did you think I'd perhaps looted this house of silverware?"

Somebody in the crowd laughed, and it spread like fire. They were all laughing while Kane got redder and redder. I almost felt sorry for the guy.

I said, "Mrs. Brindley, I'll attend to that little matter now. After I have a drink. This has been a most unnerving experience."

"Meet me at my lawyer's office tomorrow," she said loudly. "I'll tell you who he is when you bring the necklace back. Of all the insufferable people I have ever encountered ..."

She glared at Kane and turned her back on him. I walked away acting as if I felt a little dizzy over the whole affair. I pushed open the door to the butler's pantry. Sheila was there, along with several kitchen helpers. As I passed Sheila, without glancing at her, I pressed the pearls into her hand.

I said, "Will someone please get me a drink of cold water?"

Sheila elbowed her way clear and went after it. I walked to a corner of the kitchen and leaned against the wall. She brought me the water. While the glass was raised to my lips, I whispered to her.

"My car is parked outside. Meet me there. I'll be awhile."

She didn't even nod, but I knew she understood what I said. I thanked her, handed back the glass and marched out through the dining room and into the reception hall. Kane was gone; the dancing had resumed. There were a few discreet stares in my direction. I walked out to the big porch. Things were too quiet. The excitement had died away too fast.

I had not intended to pass that necklace to Sheila, but something had warned me not to carry that fortune in pearls. First of all, there was Mona to remember—and what she had said about getting the necklace. I'd half expected to find her present at the party. When she didn't put in an appearance, my suspicions became aroused. Besting Kane might only be a preliminary. If I had Mona to contend with, I didn't want to be caught with the pearls on me. Anyway, since my arrival I had known I'd be an idiot to try to steal them.

The Fairweather estate was out of the city, covered a good many acres of ground and had a big driveway circling the front of the house. As I started to cross it, a man in a chauffeur's cap stepped out from between two cars and touched his forehead in what was supposed to be a salute.

"Mrs. Brindley has ordered me to drive you, sir," he said.

"Thanks," I told him. "I'll use my own car."

He moved up beside me very fast and poked me in the ribs with a gun. "Mrs. Brindley don't like it if I disobey orders, chum. Start walking. That black sedan straight ahead."

"What the hell is this?" I demanded.

"That all depends on you," he replied. We were beside the car and he opened the rear door. "Get in, friend."

I hesitated, turning my back to the open car door. "Now look here…" I started to say.

A pair of enormous hands came out of the car, grabbed my shoulders and pulled me back. I lost my balance, but those hands held me up. I was dragged into the car and thrown onto the seat. The man with the persuasive methods was a real brute. He could have torn me apart if he wanted to.

"Sit still and keep your goddam yap shut," he told me. I decided it would be wise to obey him. He glanced at the other man. "Come on, Paul, get this crate outta here. We ain't got all night."

Paul, the man in the chauffeur's cap, grinned, removed the cap and tossed it under the nearest car. He got behind the wheel, backed out and made a fast turn. In a moment we were rolling down the driveway. Nobody said anything. We turned onto the highway, but I noticed it was to the left and not back toward the city.

"May I ask a question?" I said.

The big guy grinned. "Sure, pal. Why not?"

"Where are you taking me?"

"That's a reasonable question," he said. "You want an answer? Okay, so you get it."

I wasn't prepared for the punch that landed high on my stomach. It was short but powerful, and it sent pain shooting all through my middle. I bent over, grabbing at my stomach. The big guy clipped me on the back of the neck, and I feel over and landed wedged between the back seat and the front. He grabbed a handful of hair and hauled me up into a sitting position.

"Any more questions?" he asked.

I wondered if I could get in one good sucker punch, but I decided against it. I was already reduced to about half strength, thanks to those blows, and this guy looked as if a sledge hammer wouldn't make much of an impression on him.

He cuffed me across the mouth. Just a light, gentle tap. It sent a rivulet of blood between my teeth and knocked me dizzy.

"Now I'll ask one," he said. "Where is it?"

"Do you mean the necklace?" I said tightly.

"What else? Hand it over."

"I haven't got it."

"Aw now, you seem to like trouble, Sloan." He walloped me on my already sore belly, doubled me up and slammed me again on the back of the neck. This time I almost blacked out. He hauled me back and started searching me. He had a quaint way of doing it. His hands were very big and my pockets were not, so he simply ripped them open. After I looked like a scarecrow in a corn field, he settled back.

"Well, what do y' know? Hey, Paul—he ain't got it on him. What now?"

"Wait until we come to a good place," Paul said, without turning his head. "If he ain't got it, he knows where it is. I wouldn't put it past him to have shoved it down behind the car seat."

The big guy liked that idea too. He grabbed my chin in one hand and squeezed. I could feel teeth move under the pressure.

"Are you playin' games with me, boy? Come on—is Paul right?"

"No," I said. "I gave the damned thing back."

The big guy relaxed a bit. "Imagine—he gave it back. I thought you was a big shot crook, Sloan. I ain't never heard of no crook giving the haul back."

"There were cops in the house. I never stole the necklace. Who sent you guys, anyway?"

"He's lying," Paul opined. "We'll see."

He turned down a dark, narrow road, followed it a mile and then stopped. The big guy opened the door, stepped out and then reached inside. He wound an arm around my neck and dragged me out. I'd seen wrestlers apply this hold, but the best of them couldn't have equaled this guy. He threw me to the ground, and I bounced when I landed.

Paul said, "You treat him too rough. Help the gent up, for God's sake. When I ask a man questions, I want to see his face."

I was dutifully hauled to my feet, and I stood there, knees shaking—not so much from fear as from weakness. I'd been tossed around too much. Suddenly the big one grabbed both my wrists, yanked them behind me and stuck a knee into the small of my back. Paul punched me low, said, "Where is it?" didn't even wait for an answer and punched again. He kept this up for a couple of minutes. The big guy was laughing.

"Hey, Paul," he said, "lemme take him. You ain't got no more steam than a gnat's whisker."

"No," Paul shouted. "I don't want him killed. I'll wear him down."

He started the punching again. I knew I couldn't take too much of this. No matter what the big guy thought, those were not the blows of a gnat's whisker I was getting. My stomach heaved over once. I got sick, and they both laughed. In a couple of minutes it all started again. I just went slack, my knees buckling under me. If they were going to kill me, let them get it over with. I was done—finished.

The big man let go of me and I crumpled. I could have moved, but I didn't want them to know it. Paul put his foot against my chest and toppled me over backwards. Then he stood on my chest for a couple of seconds, jumped up and down once and asked me what I'd done with the necklace. I didn't utter a sound, although I felt like screaming.

The big man went over to the car, hauled out the back seat and flung it to the ground. Paul got sore.

"You big ox, I paid better'n two grand for that car. Whaddya wanta do, bust it up on me?"

I turned my head. From where I lay, I could see the back of the car and the license plate was brightly illuminated. I memorized those numbers, although I didn't have much hope that I'd ever be able to use this information. The more I'd seen this big goon work, the more I pegged him as the brutal killer of Marty Carroll and that jewel thief they'd found a couple of days later. I thought I must look something like Marty had when I found him. My ribs ached; there was pain shooting all around my stomach. The taste of bile gagged me, and my head hurt as if it had been in a vise.

Paul came back and kicked me experimentally in the ribs a few times. "Well, he ain't no use to us any more. Y'know, it would be funny if he had given that necklace back to the dame. Imagine, making us work like this for nothing."

The big guy said, "I dunno—maybe I should fix him for keeps."

"She didn't give us any orders like that," Paul objected. "Maybe she wouldn't want it that way."

She! Instantly Mona flashed into my tortured mind. This was her way of getting back at me. The rotten little—

Paul said, "Let him lay. What the hell's the difference? It'll be hours before he hits town if he ever does. Come on, we're getting outta here."

They were leaving me. Relief flooded my brain, but I anticipated something good just a trifle too quickly. Paul drew back his foot and kicked me under the chin. That was all I needed. The stars staring down at me went into a tailspin and then blotted out.

I was considerably surprised to find them still in the sky when I opened my eyes again. Insects were chirping. Each chirp felt like the blow of a hammer against an anvil. I shouted something, and the racket was cut off as if a sound track had broken.

I pulled myself into a sitting position and wondered how a man could ache this much and still want to be alive. I rolled over on my side, got a knee under me and tried to get up. I couldn't make it. I fell back, spread myself out and just lay there until I could feel the strength flowing back into my muscles.

It had been quite a night.

CHAPTER TEN

I T TOOK ME half an hour to thumb a ride to town. A couple of cars slowed down, but the drivers took one look at me and stepped on it. Finally an old lady in a rickety sedan pulled up. Maybe she couldn't see well; maybe she figured she was so ancient nothing could harm her. At any rate, she rode me all the way to the river and kept up an incessant chatter about such things as night traffic, her grandchildren's hoola hoops, and a man she had known who drunk himself to death. She harped on that last matter so much I thought she had noticed what I looked like, all right, and was trying to give me an object lesson. I thanked her, headed for the subway, but decided I might get pinched before I got very far and called a taxi. Those goons hadn't taken my money, though I couldn't think why.

The cab took me to my hotel and I had the driver wait. I hurried upstairs. Kane's boys wouldn't be watching me now. He'd have called them off earlier having thought that right about this time I'd be peering out of a cell. I took off what was left of the tux and cleaned up a bit, though no manner of spit and polish could remove the bruises on my face. Then I went down to the street and had the cab driver take me to my office. Again I told him to wait.

I unlocked the lobby door, signed the lobby book, went to my office and opened the safe. From it, I took a .45 Colt automatic and shoved it into my hip pocket. Next I ran through several inexpensive cultured pearl necklaces I owned until I found one which vaguely resembled Mrs. Brindley's. Then I sat down at my desk, picked up the phone and dialed the Motor Vehicle Department.

I said, "This is Captain Jack Kane, Police. I want the owner of a black sedan, license plate 3XC4601. I want it right away. Hit and run case."

I wrote down the name and address as it was given to me. Paul Stoker, 2297 Camp Street, a downtown address which had seen better days. I had the same cab driver take me there. By then I'd run up a sizable bill. I paid him off with a good tip and he was a happy man. This one job paid enough to let him go home early. I was glad somebody was happy.

I wasn't. I found that Paul Stoker lived in a four-story walk-up apartment house. There was no mistake about it. His car was parked in front of the place.

I walked in, found his name on the rusty mail boxes and climbed four flights, damning each step. Partly because I was mad, mostly because I ached from head to foot and climbing stairs increased the pain. I pulled the big gun, held it in my right hand and used the knuckles of that same hand to rap on the door. Then I slanted the gun at just about where I figured Stoker's head would be when he opened up.

I heard him coming toward the door. He must have had an easy conscience because he opened right up. The gun was about an inch from his nose.

I said, "Step back and leave the door alone, you punk, or I'll blow the top of your goddam head off."

He knew I meant it. He stepped back fast and raised his hands as high as his shoulders. He'd turned a chic gray-green.

"Now look, Mr. Sloan," he said. The 'mister' part got me. "I didn't mean no harm. Spike, he wanted to finish you off, but I wouldn't let him."

I swung the gun and smacked him over the mouth with it. Then I pushed him back until he fell against a cot and landed on it. I hit him again, drawing the muzzle of the gun down from the middle of his forehead, over his nose clear down to the chin. It left a big red welt.

"When I'm pushed around, I push back," I said. "You can have your choice of two things. Tell me who sent you or get your face plastered against the wall behind you. I don't care much which."

He held up one hand quickly, as if it could stave off another pistol whipping. "Now look, Mr. Sloan, you know how these things are."

"I know I'm a prospective killer," I said.

"You can't expect me to rat. You wouldn't if you were me. Now would you, Mr. Sloan?"

"I don't know. It might depend on the kind of treatment I got. Like this, for instance."

I smacked him with the gun again. This time the corner of his mouth cracked open, and blood ran down over his chin. He looked great to me.

"You'll kill me anyway!" he shouted. "You're crazy!"

"Okay, Stoker. We might as well get it over with."

I stepped back two paces, slanted the gun down at his heart region and started squeezing the trigger. He let out a howl of anguish.

"Don't shoot, for Christ's sake, Mr. Sloan. I'll talk."

"That's better, but you'd better hurry up."

"I don't know the name of the dame. I don't know where she came from neither, but she's some dish. You take just a look at her, and you'll say she's a beautiful lay and—"

"Skip the sex appeal," I said. "Where can I find her?"

"I don't know that either. You gotta believe me. I met her only once—in a fancy café. Listen, Sloan, just to prove I'm leveling, she's taking over the town. Yeah—every smart cookie in your racket has gotta work with her or … or …"

He stopped short, realizing he'd said too much.

"Or somebody will get killed—like Marty Carroll. Who killed him? Was it the big guy?"

"Yeah. Yeah, Spike don't know his own strength. He was told to go see Marty and make him understand he had to join up. Marty wouldn't and Spike got rough. I wasn't there...."

"The hell you weren't. This woman—who told her about you?"

"I don't know ..."

I carved a neat gouge on the top of his head. It must have felt like an earthquake to him. He yelled and clapped both hands to his head and swore he didn't know. I half believed him.

"But somebody did," I insisted. "She's a newcomer to town, isn't she?"

He got some of his old zing back. I watched him lick his lips. "You see this tomato once, and you don't ever forget her. She's built, this broad."

"And you don't know who suggested you to her?"

"That's the truth, Mr. Sloan. She just called me up and her voice is like honey. I figured it was some kind of a date she wanted, and when I saw her, boy, I started heating up, but she soon cooled me down. That's when I got orders to watch that estate, and when you came out to grab you and get them pearls."

I said, "Let me describe this dream dish, Stoker. She's about five feet ten, with jet black hair and eyes. She's got olive skin, a build like a dream. You're correct about that ..."

He shook his head and winced. After what I'd handed him, the slightest movement must have hurt—I hoped.

"You got it all wrong, Mr. Sloan. She's a blonde. Her hair is so damn blonde it don't look real and she's got blue eyes. Kind of a baby face, but she's tough too. If she'd have told me to jump off the Empire State and land on my head, I'd have done it if I thought maybe I'd get a crack at her first."

I didn't show it, but I was stumped. Stoker wouldn't be lying—not now. And no beauty parlor could have changed Mona over into a blue-eyed blonde. This had to be someone else, and the set-up didn't ring true.

"When are you supposed to see her again, Stoker?" I asked.

"She said she'd contact me. Hell, I don't even know her name."

"Was anybody with her?"

"She was all alone."

"Where can I find Spike?"

He gave a sharp shiver. "Listen, Mr. Sloan, you don't want to go near him. He's so dumb he's dangerous. Even with that big gun he'd try to grab you and if he did, he'd kill you. Stay away from him."

"Where can I find him?"

"I'm telling you, it's no good. Besides, he'd tear my head off if he thought I squealed."

"Having Spike tear your head off is a problem to consider in the future, but unless you tell me now, you won't have any future."

"He lives in a crumb joint on West Eighth Street. Number Fifteen-twenty. You ain't gonna tell him I sent you..."

I said, "Get up, Stoker. On your feet."

"What—you going to do?"

"On your feet." I started raising the gun and he jumped up.

"Give me a break, Mr. Sloan. I saved your life."

"Get down on the floor," I ordered. "Flat on your back."

"Sure. Anything you say, Mr. Sloan."

He flopped quickly and rolled over on his back. I stepped up to him and pulled one foot back. "Next time you have a lot of fun kicking a guy on the chin, I want you to know what it feels like. And next time we meet, Stoker, I'll kill you."

He let out half a bleat before my foot found contact with his chin. His eyes glazed and he became quiet. I searched him, just in case he had anything which might point to the strange blonde. His pockets held nothing of interest and the dresser drawers contained only clothing. I walked out, feeling quite a lot better.

Sheila would be going quietly nuts by now, so I couldn't delay going back any longer. It took a taxi forty minutes to make the trip, even at this time of night, but as it pulled into the long drive to the house, I saw that the party was still in full swing. I paid off the driver, took a quick look around and went over to where my new car was parked. When I opened the door, Sheila flung her arms around my neck. She'd been crying. I could see how tear-stained her make-up was.

"Mike, oh, Mike, I've been so damned worried. You were gone so long that I ..." She saw my face for the first time. "You've been hurt, darling. Mike, did Jack do that?"

"I'm not certain who was responsible," I said, "but it's a good thing I gave you the necklace, because that's what they were after. Do you still have it?"

"Yes—of course."

"That's great, baby. I'm going inside—only be a couple of minutes and then I'll take you home."

"Please hurry, Mike," she implored. I knew what was worry-ing her. If Kane got home before she did, he'd ask a lot of ques-tions. I decided to talk about that later.

I hurried into the house and sought out Mrs. Brindley. In the full light she saw my face immediately. "Mike, what in the world happened to you?"

"Somebody tried to snatch your necklace," I said.

"They tried to steal it from you?"

"That's right."

She said, "Mike, I don't care if they got it. Perhaps that impossible detective will claim you marked yourself up that way to account for the loss of the pearls. I won't believe that ..."

I reached into my pocket and pulled out the phony string. "Thanks, Mrs. Brindley, because they didn't get them. Here they are, all repaired and ready."

She wasn't fooled for one second. She knew those were phonies because of the difference in the clasp.

I said, in a low voice, "I've got to talk to you alone. Everything is okay, including the pearls. Let's go back to that little room."

We made our way there and I closed the door. "Thanks for not making a fuss when I handed you that phony string, Mrs. Brindley."

"I was astounded, Mike, but I suppose you have a reason."

"A good one. When they didn't find the necklace on me, they'll assume you have it. So—put this one on. If anybody holds you up, let them have it. If you'll come outside with me, I'll show you the real one—give it to you if you like, though I wouldn't advise that."

"Keep it, Mike. I trust you. So I'm going to be held up."

"I'm not sure, but it certainly seems as if you might. If you wish, I'll arrange a guard …."

She shook her head and smiled, "No thanks. It sounds exciting, and besides I can take good care of myself. Thank you, Mike, for what you've done—but what shall we do about that policeman?"

"I'm going to sue."

"Good—so am I. My lawyer is Oliver Parks. You'll find his address in the phone book. I'll meet you at his office tomorrow afternoon at two. I'm paying all the expenses. This is on me, Mike."

I bussed her on the cheek, and she laughed and whacked me one on the rump. I helped her put the phony necklace on, and we went back to the ballroom where things were beginning to die off. I left her there, returned to my car and drove it away fast. Sheila said nothing until I started to talk.

"Baby, I can't see your husband having anything to do with this attack on me. It would be simply too crazy for him to try. Besides, I understand it was directed by a woman."

"A woman? Mike, that's fantastic."

"In this business nothing is fantastic, beautiful."

"Jack will be in an ugly mood even if he finds me there and if he doesn't …"

I said, "After you go in, I'll wait around front for a while. If he starts anything, walk out and I'll be there."

She touched my cheek. Her hands were cool and smooth. When we were near her apartment she gave me the genuine pearls.

"They're so lovely, Mike. I hate to let them go."

I grinned at her. "Then you'll have a string equally as lovely. I have them in stock, and I can make up a necklace in no time."

"No, Mike. I wouldn't dare. Jack …"

"Damn him," I said vehemently. "Every time I think of something good for us, he stands in the way. Baby, are you sure you want to go through with this? I mean, wrecking his career?"

"I don't care what you do. Jack means nothing to me any more."

"He's going to get it from two directions. Mrs. Brindley is hopping mad, and she's going to sue, too."

Sheila settled back and closed her eyes. "I wish I could care, Mike. I married Jack, and I loved him once, but he isn't the same man any more. Sometimes I think he enjoys the power of his position above anything else. But he loves money too—or what it can buy." She broke off, then said, "There is only one thing I'm happy about."

"I hope it concerns me," I said.

"It does. I'm glad you didn't steal that necklace."

I braked the car and turned it toward the curb, stopped and kissed her soundly. "If you say so, baby, I'm finished with that racket."

"No, Mike. I won't give you orders. I'm only thinking that my life with Jack has been one of constant worry. I'd hate to have history repeat itself with you. I'm the worrying type, you see."

I smiled at her. "I'm finished with the game, Sheila, but it's possible the game isn't finished with me. There's something cock-eyed going on. Two of my friends have been murdered. I know who killed them and I know why, but I'm not sure what's behind it. I have an idea they may pick on me next. If they do, I'm going to take them, baby."

"I know how you feel, darling. I've got to run now. I hate to. Each time is harder, but some day soon, I hope, we won't have to say good night ever again."

She got out of the car and hurried toward the entrance of her building. I sat there and smoked three cigarettes, giving her plenty of time if she wanted to come back to me. She didn't, so I drove around to my office. Carrying that necklace with me was tempting the fates too much. I wanted to put it in a safer place.

Again, I unlocked the big glass door in the lobby, scribbled my name in the after-hours book, rode the self-service elevator to my floor and let myself into my office. I went straight to the safe, opened it and put the necklace inside. When the door closed and the dial spun under my fingers, I felt much better.

There was a bottle of brandy in my bottom drawer. I fished it out, started to get up and fetch a glass and then said to hell with it. I tilted the bottle and drank. My stomach was still sore, and the fiery liquid didn't help at first. But after a couple of shots the pain went away and I began feeling very good.

One thing puzzled me. What had Kane been after when he searched me that second time? He'd looked for something defi-nite. It was no hunch that made him frisk me. He knew I wouldn't carry a gun on a job so that couldn't be it.

I should have been tired. It was two in the morning and I'd been through a lot, but I had never felt more wide awake. I had another slug out of the bottle, lit a cigarette and propped my feet on the desk. There was a great deal to think about. Captain Kane, Sheila, the mysterious blonde number, but most of all I wanted to plan something of a future for Sheila. A first-rate future such as she deserved.

I knew I was done with stealing. I'd seen it coming for some time now, and I only needed an incentive like Sheila to hurry things along. But until I found out what lay behind a couple of murders and a beating up I'd taken, I meant to stay around. Besides, there was my scheme to make Kane so disgusted he'd be glad to let Sheila go. She didn't know it, but that civil action I intended to institute against him would be a great big club. I'd wreck him first and then if he stood in our way, I'd use that club.

Something scraped against the door of the outer office. My feet came off the desk fast and quietly. I stood up, whisked the .45 out of my pocket and killed the desk lamp. I walked toward the door to the reception room, lined myself up beside it and held the gun ready.

Whoever it was used a key. I heard the outer door open, close after a couple of seconds and then someone moved across the floor toward my private office. There was very little light, only that which came from the street. When you're fourteen floors above the sidewalks, that light doesn't amount to much. It only enabled me to distinguish a slim figure coming through the doorway.

I could have whacked him one with the gun and I was half tempted to, but that would mean waking him up afterwards. So I just took one step out from the wall, wound my left arm around the guy's neck and drove the gun into the small of his back. I drew a sharp yell. A feminine yell.

CHAPTER ELEVEN

I TURNED ON the lights and then let go of her. Mona was a pasty white under that olive complexion of hers. She grabbed at my arm for support. I dropped the gun into my side coat pocket.

"Mike," she gasped, "you scared ten years off my life."

"What are you doing here?" I asked. "And while I'm on the subject, I think you'd better leave your key."

"Oh, Mike, don't be sore at me. I waited at your hotel for hours and when you didn't come, I got so damn worried. I came over here because I remembered that you never kept a haul intact any longer than necessary and I thought you might be in the workshop breaking down Mrs. Brindley's necklace."

"I didn't get it," I said. "The lay wasn't right. Kane was there— in force."

She moved closer to me. Mona was quite a woman. There was no denying that, and I was tempted to crush her to me with both arms. She had that sultry look in her eyes too—the kind she always got when things were exactly right and she wanted me to want her. I walked over and sat on the edge of the desk.

"So you came here because you were worried. You didn't seem worried when you started smashing up the office."

"I was a fool, Mike. You knew I'd be back."

"I didn't even think about it, if there's any consolation for you in that statement. I've been too busy."

"With Sheila Kane?"

"Among other things. It's no concern of yours."

She came up to me quickly. "Mike, have you forgotten what we meant to one another? Have you forgotten all our days—and nights?"

"I have trouble with my memory. Especially when a girl starts throwing things. It gives me amnesia."

She bit her lip. "I'm not going to get sore, Mike. You can't make me. I came because I have something to tell you. It would be a lot better for both of us if we were back where we used to be, but I'm not begging. I do have your welfare at heart."

"Yeah," I said. "What are you measuring me for, a knife in the back?"

She went around and sat in my chair behind the desk. She put her feet on it, pulled her dress high and gave me a good look at legs I used to think were absolutely marvelous. I still thought so, but I kept that fact to myself.

"Things have changed, Mike. In town, I mean. They changed awfully fast."

I said, "Yeah, I noticed they were digging another hole in the middle of Thirty-fourth Street."

She didn't smile. "Somebody has taken over every fence, fin-german and smart thief, Mike. If you want to work this town, you've got to belong."

"I'm not a joiner," I said.

"You'll be dead if you fight them. Marty Carroll tried it. So did another man. They're both dead."

"Come up with something new, baby. I even know who killed them."

Her feet came off the desk fast. "You do? Then you've already been approached..."

"Take another look at my face, Mona. That's changed too. A pair of goons did that. They got nothing for their pains, but I came away with souvenirs."

"Then you know how ruthless they can be, Mike."

"I have a pretty good idea. How are you mixed up in this?"

"They still thought I worked with you, and that they could reach you through me best. I was asked to meet someone in a cocktail room and that's when I got the lowdown."

"Was this someone a gorgeous blonde number with blue eyes and a baby face? Perhaps a shape to make a guy drool."

"Mike, have you met her too?"

"No—not yet. When I do, I'll turn her fanny as blue as her eyes."

"Oh, Mike, you don't know what you're saying. I tell you this is no fake. She has most of the good crooks in town sewed up already. It's become a syndicate. They're going to strip every dowager and movie star down to their gold teeth. By now I don't think there's a smart operator in town who doesn't belong. Those who hesitated about joining were shown the error of their ways."

This was very interesting. A combine of all slick jewel thieves, incorporating, of course, the best fences and finger-men. I'd have wanted no part of it even if I hadn't already decided to give up the racket. But I wanted to know more. "So they contacted you. What was the proposition?"

"It's very simple. You join the others. They set up the job, see to it a maximum amount of loot will be there for the taking. They case the place, get rid of any obstacles. You go in, help yourself and leave. You turn the take over, and, after it's converted, you get your share of the cash."

I laughed at her. "You know how I've always worked, Mona. I don't split with anybody."

"You'll have to from here on if you want to stay in business, Mike."

"Have you joined them?"

She tossed her head. "They don't want me except as an understudy to you. I'm just delivering a message."

"I'd like to meet this blonde."

"That can be arranged. I'm supposed to take you to her."

"Ah—good. When?"

"They'll send the word."

"So I'm supposed to be taking orders already. Let her come to see me."

Mona got up and walked toward me. "I'm warning you, darling, you're not playing games with these people. There's money behind them—and muscle, too, if muscle is necessary."

"I'll think it over."

She stepped up to me and suddenly put her arms around my neck. Her head was tilted invitingly, her lips waiting.

I felt her body pushed hard against mine and, quite out of force of habit, I put my own arms around her.

"Let's go in the back room, Mike."

"Uh-uh. I told you, we were through."

"I don't believe you." She reached my lips with hers and crushed them. My spine tingled. I'd be a liar if I said she didn't affect me. "I've come back to you, Mike."

I forced her arms down and stepped back. "No sale, baby."

"You couldn't put me off if I really went after you, Mike. You never could put any woman off." She threw her hat onto a chair, followed it with the light jacket she wore and then quickly unzipped her dress. She peeled it off. The dress was carelessly dropped to the floor and next she removed the slip too and stood there in front of me in panties and a bra. Her hair was wild, her eyes were hot and her smile and expression sure and eager.

"Now stay away from me," she challenged.

I blinked a couple of times. She started swaying, taunting me, laughing at me with her eyes.

I gave a lunge, and she laughed shrilly and grabbed me hard. My hands slid down her smooth sides, followed the contours of her rounded hips. Then I raised my hand about two feet and brought it down in a sharp, painful slap that caught her squarely across the fanny.

She gave a sharp yelp. I pushed her roughly away from me, went to the desk and lit a cigarette. It wobbled slightly between my lips, and it tasted of her lipstick, but I stood there, oblivious to her charms.

It took her a few seconds to realize I meant all this. Then she started swearing. She swore in at least three languages. I didn't understand the words, but the meaning was clear enough. Mona hadn't climbed quite as far out of the slime as I'd thought.

When I had enough of that, I started moving toward her with a doubled fist. She remembered that crack on the jaw and retreated quickly, grabbing her clothes on the way. I watched her get back into them. She didn't say anything. Dressed now, she jammed on her hat and walked to the door. There, she turned around.

"I have to take you to see Maxine. They'll kill me if I don't bring you, and nothing but such a threat would bring me back to you. I'm not forgetting, Mike. I have a long memory. I'm not used to being turned down."

She departed stormily, slamming the door. Then she opened it again and stuck her head inside. "I must have the key to get the lobby door open. I'll drop it on the sidewalk outside. If somebody finds it and uses it, I'll be very happy. I hope they steal everything you own."

The door slammed again. I more or less tottered over to my chair, sat down and picked up the brandy bottle. I didn't put it down for a long time.

I felt as if I'd looked down the barrel of a murderer's gun for about an hour. If Mona had kissed me once more—just the slightest additional tease—I'd have succumbed. After that episode, I figured I could give up smoking and drinking and even make myself brush my teeth after every meal. Nobody had more will power than me, and I wished that the shaking would stop.

After awhile, I went down to the lobby door and found her key flung against the doorsill. I didn't feel much like going home so I returned to the office, went into the workshop and stretched out on the divan. What a sucker I was. For a girl—a married one, at that—whom I trusted and wanted, I was now sleeping alone. Mona would forever be a danger to me. With her around, I might let myself go, and I knew that Sheila would put up with that only to the suspicion stage. She'd been through enough with Jack Kane. I told myself she was worth it, though. Worth any sacrifice I could make, and, brother, I'd just made one.

Things were in such a damned mess I didn't quite know where to begin. First, I'd decided to get out of the business and now some blonde was telling me I had to work for her. There seemed to be no middle ground. If I quit, I'd better leave town. The blonde would have more than one Spike working for her. I knew what that goon was capable of and I didn't want to meet any more of his kind unless I had a gun in my fist.

I toyed with the idea of dropping everything, picking up Sheila and just taking a little trip—for about six years. It would be very easy to do, except that two different parties might decide they didn't like it. Between Kane and his cops, the blonde and her goons, I wouldn't last long as a free agent.

The blonde interested me. I wanted to know more about her. Apparently nobody saw her unless she made the date. Well, she would, and Mona was too scared not to let me know when and where. Things didn't worry me much, but I was a little surprised to find that I was holding that .45 in my fist when I woke up the next morning.

I had an electric razor in the office, so I cleaned up, sat still long enough to smoke a couple of cigarettes and figure out my next move. It was obvious. Protect what I had. If things became too hot, I'd need all the dough I could lay my hands on. So I fished a briefcase out of the steel locker and filled it with diamonds, rubies, emeralds and little bars of gold. I added what money I had hidden around the office, and I was half tempted to toss Mrs. Brindley's pearls into the sack, too. But I didn't. I put them in my pocket. The one closest to where I carried the .45.

I went around to my bank, signed into the safe deposit department and got out one of their big boxes. I dumped the contents of the briefcase into it, put the box away temporarily and then went to three different banks where I cleaned out my accounts and got negotiable securities from safe deposit boxes I rented in those other banks. One more visit to the box I'd selected to hold my entire assets and then I felt much better. Not even the blonde could get at that box.

I suddenly realized I was hungry so I stopped in at a place I knew and had lunch. It was that late in the day. Just before two, I looked up Attorney Oliver Parks, went to his office and found Mrs. Brindley waiting there for me.

I shook hands with the lawyer and then I gave Mrs. Brindley her real pearls. "I didn't take time to repair them," I said. "Perhaps you'd feel safer having someone else do the job. I'd like that cheap string back though, if you don't mind."

She laughed curtly. "They were taken from me in the lobby of my apartment house last night—by two men, one of whom stuck a knife against my throat. But he was a gentleman. He only scratched me with it once when I called him a low-lifed bastard."

I grinned. Mrs. Brindley and I understood one another very well indeed. The lawyer was all business.

"I think," he said, "that any jury will decide you cannot be a thief, Mr. Sloan, when they learn you actually had a fortune in pearls on you for almost twenty-four hours and brought them safely back to their rightful owner."

I said, "Hell, what do I want them for?"

Which was at least the second biggest lie in the world.

"I understand you wish to file suit against Captain Kane, the officers who were with him last night, against the Police Department and the city. I shall be delighted to handle your case."

"Good," I said. "I don't so much mind being called a crook in private, but in front of an audience composed largely of friends and customers—well, you begin the action. Handle it on a contingency basis if you like or I'll pay any retainer you wish."

He smiled thinly. This guy would take Kane over. I bad an idea he didn't like cops either. He said, "Mrs. Brindley retains me on an annual basis and there will be no talk about fees at the present time. Now I want all the facts."

I gave them to him while he made a lot of notes on small scraps of paper. When he had all he wanted, he shook hands with me. "I'll have the papers served this afternoon. I presume you won't object to publicity in this matter."

"The more the better. You handle it," I said. "I'm too biased."

Mrs. Brindley and I walked out together. She said, "You know, Mike, I'm glad this happened. I haven't had so much fun in a long time."

"It might not be so funny when we go into court," I said. "However, we do hold all the cards. Now about the pearls. Before somebody else gets a happy thought about grabbing them, suppose we take a run over to your bank and put them on ice."

"A good idea, Mike. You think of everything."

When we reached the outside of the building, a tall rangy young fellow came over. He smelled copper four miles off with the wind in the wrong direction.

"Good afternoon, Mr. Sloan," he said. "Inspector McDermott would like to see you."

"What?" I asked. "No patrol wagon?"

He grinned sheepishly. "This isn't a pinch, Mr. Sloan. It's just that the inspector wants to see you, and he knew you'd be around this building today and asked me to keep an eye out for you."

"All right," I said. "But first, Mrs. Brindley here is carrying around a mint of pearls. We were going to the bank with them. I'd like it if you tagged along—a few steps behind. Somebody's tried to swipe these pearls a couple of times already."

"Nobody will swipe them now," he vowed.

I winked at Mrs. Brindley. "We've got them eating out of our hands already."

"Do you think the inspector wants to make trouble, Mike?"

"No. If I'm right, he'll begin apologizing for Kane."

"Well, you call my attorney if he gets out of line, Mike. You've done me a favor, and I don't intend to see them harm you."

We put the necklace away in her safe deposit vault while the cop from Inspector McDermott's office watched. I put Mrs. Brindley into a cab, sent her home and called another one. The cop with me was a likeable kid, a little green-eared still, but it wouldn't be long before he'd be chasing guys like me and probably doing quite well at it. We kept up meaningless chatter all the way.

McDermott's office was in keeping with his rank. It had two desks in it, otherwise it was equipped with that same ugly oak furniture city buyers always manage to dig up somewhere. I knew McDermott slightly. He was a good cop—all cop, but square—a big man with a ruff of white hair on top of his head, like a misplaced collar. He motioned me to a chair.

"I'm glad you could drop over, Sloan. Sit down. You had a little trouble last night, I hear."

"It didn't seem trivial at the time, Inspector."

"Oh, I know. Some of the boys are impulsive at times. I think we can straighten it all out."

I said, "You'll have to talk to my lawyer. He's Mrs. Brindley's attorney also, and he intends to serve the papers today. Kane isn't getting away with this."

McDermott flushed slightly. "Now listen, Sloan. If you were an ordinary citizen and an ordinary mistake had been made, I wouldn't have to say this, but you're exactly what Kane swears you are. We all know that."

I laughed at him. "Call in a couple of disinterested people and repeat that, Inspector. If it keeps on, I'll get rich by legally raiding the city treasury."

He calmed down some. "Then you're actually going through with it?"

"Stick around this afternoon and you'll find out."

"Think it over, Sloan. We might be able to make it tough for you in court. Maybe we know more than you think about jobs you've pulled."

That called for another laugh. "If you had so much as a parking violation on me, I'd be sitting here getting hell. That line won't work, Inspector."

"No," he said, "perhaps not, now. But something will."

I walked out. Kane was nowhere about. As I passed the main desk, a seedy little guy with a fistful of envelopes was asking where he could find Kane. Mrs. Brindley's lawyer had wasted little time.

CHAPTER TWELVE

I WAS CLIMBING into a gray flannel suit early that evening when Mona called on the phone. Her tone was cold as ice.

"That light-haired person will be at the Café Françoise at eight sharp. I'm to tell you that."

"Ah," I said. "The summons. Can you make contact with her?"

"I might."

"Tell my blonde friend I'll be at my office from eight until nine. Those aren't my usual business hours, but I'll be glad to oblige a prospective customer."

"She won't like it, Mike."

"Do you care?"

"No, damn you! I hope she blows your skull open. I'll tell her."

The phone slammed in my ear. I grinned, hung up and went back to dressing.

I set out a silver tray with a decanter of whisky, glasses, a seltzer bottle and a thermos jug of ice cubes. It reminded me of the days when I had a fifty thousand dollar bit of merchandise to sell to some dowager who was more impressed with surroundings and courtesy than what I had to show her.

At five minutes of eight someone tried the outer door, found it open and came in. I was wondering what this gorgeous number who had impressed Paul Stoker so much actually looked like. It was no blonde who came into my private office. Two men, one of them holding a gun, marched in. The one with the gun stuck it in my direction while the other went all through the place. He even checked for hidden microphones. I had a lot of fun watching him. Then I was searched, but the .45 was in the vault. I'd been a bit worried about a rambunctious Captain Kane raiding the office because I had no permit to keep a gun.

Neither man said a word. Satisfied that I had no trap set, they backed out and I heard the door close softly. Two minutes went by. I didn't move at all. Then the door opened again and I heard lighter footsteps crossing the rug. She stopped in the doorway to pose. I thought that she was exactly the type to impress Paul Stoker.

She was blonde all right. Startlingly so, and a cross between a honey-haired number and the platinum kind. Her face looked more like it went with the platinum. She was statuesque, a trifle on the big side, but not heavy, so Paul had been right about her figure. She had a loose kind of mouth and blue eyes. They were nice eyes, except the flesh beneath them was inclined to be puffy. My flash opinion was that she'd been an extremely handsome girl, still was, but the days of her good looks were numbered.

I figured she might be quite interesting, but I couldn't place her as the tough leader of a gang of tough guys. If she was, she didn't control them by force of will. She held them in check with her shape and maybe a few promises.

"So you're Mike Sloan," she said.

I arose and bowed slightly. "Come in and sit down. Yes, I'm Mike Sloan."

"You're a son of a bitch," she said without heat. "Why didn't you come to see me?"

"Maybe I figured there'd be too many people around. Here in my office I knew we'd be alone. You're the kind of girl to be alone with."

She liked it even though she said, "To hell with that. I'm here on business."

"I'll fix you a drink," I offered.

She looked over the silver tray and its contents. "If that's bonded stuff, I'll have some—straight. No ice. No nothing."

"Exactly the way I enjoy my liquor." I went around the desk and held a chair for her. She sat down and crossed her legs. She was no Sheila, and not in Mona's class, but she wasn't bad. My interest started growing. I poured two stiff ones and handed her one. She started to sip it and then bolted half the glass. I went back to my chair behind the desk.

"I understand you have a certain proposition to make, Miss ... What was the name again?"

"Maxine. Maxine Hewitt, and that's as phony as your line, Sloan. If you didn't happen to be about the smartest operator in town, I'd have sent the boys to work you over."

"Two of them did," I said sweetly. "One remembers the incident better than the other. Now we had definite business ..."

"Okay. I'm not in this alone, you understand. There are important people behind me. We know that this town has more diamonds and gems to the square foot than anywhere else on earth, and they're easy to get at if you have the right connections."

"Indeed," I said, "they are. Go on, I'm fascinated."

"Piddling around, grabbing a hunk of ice here and another there, gets nobody noplace. Organization, that's what people like you need, Sloan. A good tight organization."

"So true," I purred.

"We've got all the fences and fingermen lined up and most of the actual thieves, like you."

"A naughty word," I chided. "I prefer operator."

"Are you, by any chance, trying to make a joke, Sloan?"

"Why, I'm listening very eagerly to all you have to say, Maxine. You're a very lovely girl. It's a wonder I can concentrate."

She pouted, caught hold of herself and went into a tough act.

"I could have you taken care of, Sloan. Maybe you'd like a trip to the river?"

"No—I definitely wouldn't."

"Then shut up and listen. I told you we'd taken over. You're one of the few holdouts, but I admit you're also one of the best in the business. We want you to step in line."

"And what does it get me?"

"We line up the jobs, case them, finger the stuff and the people involved. Everything is all set. You just walk in and do your stuff. Doesn't that sound like a good proposition?"

"It does. How about the payoff?"

"You turn the take over to me. It'll be appraised and sold quickly for the best prices. We have that end of it sewed up, too. You'll be given a fair shake..."

"Approximately how much? After all, I'm a business man."

"Twenty-five per cent to you because you're important."

"But I make it sixty per cent of the actual, not the appraised value right now. I don't need the kind of help you offer, so why should I join simply to lose more than half of my take? You've got to do better than that, baby."

"You heard my offer. Take it or you're out of business. I mean it, Sloan. I'll show you I do."

I said, "I've had experience with your men and methods and I don't like them." I got up and walked around the desk to stand looking down at her. Those were certainly nice legs. I acted purely on impulse. I tilted her head back, and kissed her full on the lips. For just an instant I felt her respond, but then she was ice again. Blonde ice. She stood up quickly and took a swing at me. I ducked it and laughed.

"Come now, Maxine, my technique isn't as bad as that. If we're going to be partners, why not make it friendly partners? I know you hate formality. A girl with your looks and figure must."

She backed away from me. "What makes you think I'd fall for you?"

"Nothing. I don't expect you to, baby. But I like beautiful women. One like you could tempt me to make decisions that I wouldn't ordinarily consider."

"Say it," she challenged. "You think I'm a promiscuous bitch and I can be had for the reaching. Well, think again. Maybe I can be had, but not by your lousy methods. I'll give you twenty-four hours to make up your mind about joining us. After that—well, use your imagination. It must be good, because you've been undressing me with your eyes ever since I walked in here. Twenty-four hours, Sloan. Then I'll give you a ring and you'd better have an answer."

"My answer could depend on you," I said while I gave her an obvious leer.

"Damn you, Sloan, I only want you in the outfit because you're a smart crook. You mean money to me. I've given you an offer. Take it or leave it."

"If I leave it," I said, "I suppose I'd better stay out of dark alleys."

"You'd better stop living," she retorted. She stood up and hoisted the mink fur piece around her neck. All through this interview I had an idea she didn't know quite what to do. As if she wanted one thing, had been told another was best, wasn't sure about either and only wanted to get away from me for time to think it all out.

I opened the door for her. She started through, paused and turned around. "I usually get an answer, Sloan. One way or another."

"All right," I said. "The answer is no. I'm not buying."

She clucked her tongue sympathetically. "And you were such a damned good-looking guy. You know how to kiss a girl, too. Good-by, Sloan."

She walked across the outer office and I stood there, leaning against the door frame and watching her. Her face may have deteriorated some, but not her shape. She opened the hallway door and the two guys quickly moved up beside her. They all went away, and the slamming door sounded forlorn and final. I went back to my desk, smoked half a dozen cigarettes thoughtfully, had a couple of drinks and then decided to call it a day.

I already had some definite ideas about this weird set-up. Certainly Maxine didn't run it. She was merely a decorative front. Maybe she gave some of the boys a little encouragement by swinging her hips and brought them into line that way. I wanted no part of it.

I thought about taking the .45 with me but decided against it. They'd hardly have time to get set this fast, and I doubted they'd take a pot shot at me tomorrow in broad daylight. But I wasn't denying the fact that I might be in considerable danger.

When I hit the street, I took a careful look around. Nobody was watching me. It was ten o'clock, too early to go home, there was no Mona to call on, and I doubted that Sheila would be at the bar and grill. But I could try, so I shook off Kane's boys without much trouble and without letting them know they'd been deliberately shaken. I took a cab downtown and was pleasantly surprised to find Sheila at the same booth. I slid onto the seat and we held hands for a couple of minutes, not saying a word. A waiter came along and we ordered and then held hands some more.

"I didn't think you'd get here," she said. "I was almost ready to leave and I can't stay long. Jack is in a vicious mood today."

I grinned a little. "It's to be expected. Did he tell you I sued him and he was served with the papers today?"

"So that's it. No, he didn't tell me." She stopped to let the waiter put our drinks down. Then she resumed. "He came home early—around four-thirty. He growled worse than usual and all of a sudden, for no reason I knew of then, he smashed a chair. He just picked it up—one of the wooden kitchen chairs—and tore it to pieces."

"He didn't touch you?"

"No, but he kept glowering at me. Almost as if I were to blame for his troubles. Mike, he can't possibly know we meet like this, can he?"

I shook my head. "If he did, I think he'd have shown up before now and tried to take me apart like he did the chair. Sheila, is it very clear in your mind that you intend to leave him?"

"Yes—oh, yes, Mike. I want to."

"But you were in love with him once."

"Very much. He was so different in those days. Now all he wants is money and power. Essentially I think he's an honest cop and a good one, too, but there are sides to him that are black and vicious."

"It won't be long now," I said. "Just a few little matters to clean up and then we're off. I'm afraid Kane will bust everything in the apartment when he finds out."

"He mustn't," she said quickly. "I've been thinking this all out, Mike. I'll leave a note, saying I can't stand living with him any longer and that I'm going away. That's all he'll know. If he knew I went with you, he'd never stop until he found us. Mike, he might kill you."

"He might at that, baby. Or try to, at any rate. Still, he's been a cop for a long time and a cop learns just how futile murder is."

We drank, chatted awhile longer and then she had to go home. She didn't want me to even accompany her to the street. I sat there, nursing another drink. There were a lot of questions in my mind, but none of them could be answered as clearly as what Sheila meant to me and what I intended to do about it.

This goofy organization Maxine was supposed to head didn't add. Jewel thievery is a solo or, at best, a two-man stunt. It can't be done well with brute force and it takes brains and skill. A hell of a lot more than Maxine had. I wanted to get to the inside of that outfit and find out what it was composed of.

I paid the tab, went out and rode a cab home. I took the elevator up to my floor, walked down the corridor and passed the fire stairway door. I fished keys out of my pocket, turned the lock to my suite and had the door half open when somebody stuck a gun into the small of my back.

I didn't say a word. I couldn't have if I'd wanted to. All I could think of was my own foolishness. I should have known that Maxine wouldn't wait.

The man behind me said, "Walk in, pal. Do it easy. This is a big gun I got."

The voice was vaguely familiar, but I didn't turn my head. Not right then. I walked into the living room and stood there while the guy closed the door with his foot. The gun never budged out of my back. He patted my pockets, under my arms, ran his hand down my pants legs and even checked for a belly gun. When he was satisfied that I wasn't armed, he grabbed my shoulder and spun me around. Like that! I was a toy top. I could no more have resisted that muscular power than transport myself somewhere else.

His size was familiar enough, but I'd only seen Spike Tate in the dark. The voice and the size was identification enough, but I looked him over anyway so that I'd know him again on sight—if I was destined to ever see anything again. He had a broad flat face with bulging eyes like a lizard's. His skin was coarse, like that of a man who'd drunk too much for too many years. For the size of his face he had a small mouth, not wide and just a thin gash in an ugly frame.

"Where you been?" he demanded. "You been talking to the cops?"

I said, "Hello, Spike." I couldn't think of anything else and it was a dumb remark.

"I asked you a question, pal. I like to get answers. Remember? When I don't get answers, I get sore. You oughta know."

I knew all right. I said, "No cops, Spike."

"I think you're lying. I think you went to see 'em."

"I didn't talk to the cops. I never mentioned you to anyone."

"You're a wise guy. I hate wise guys. I like to smear 'em all up. I think that's what I'm gonna do to you, pal. Smear you up."

I didn't answer him or make a move. He had the muzzle of the gun right between my eyes. It looked five times as big as my .45, which was reposing nicely in the big office vault.

Spike smiled thinly. "You don't scare easy, do you, pal? You're washed up, you know that?"

"What's it going to get you, Spike?"

"A hell of a lot of satisfaction, for one thing. For another, Paul Stoker told you I knocked off Marty Carroll and that other crook. I don't like people walking around who can put the finger on me. Paul don't count because he was in on both deals and they'll fry him too. But you're different. You're the smart type. If the cops nail you, there'd be a good chance you'd make a deal with them and turn me in so you'd get off easy. I gotta fix you, pal. There just ain't no other answer."

I had to say something. Any second this big lug would fasten his fingers around my throat and start hammering me to death.

"You're playing with the wrong mob, Spike. They're using you for a sucker."

"You think so, huh?" He didn't believe it at all. Neither did I, which hardly made me sound very convincing. I tried another angle.

"If that blonde dish promised you anything, forget it. She's like a post-dated check—they never turn out the way you expect."

The mention of Maxine got him. He rolled his frog eyes and ran a fat tongue around his thin lips. "Yeah—but ain't she somethin', pal? Imagine rolling in the hay with her. And you're all wrong. She makes a promise and she keeps it."

"Did she promise you a roll in the hay, Spike?"

"It ain't right to talk about things like that," he said. "Besides, all I'm doing is wasting time. You're scared, ain't you, pal? The big moment is here. That scares you, don't it?"

I said I wasn't scared, but I hoped he didn't notice me shaking. This moron was a good killer because he never bothered to figure the odds. A kill to him was just a small piece of business. Besides, he didn't need a gun to scare people. One look at him was enough.

My voice sounded like a twenty-year-old radio with a couple of cracked tubes. "Well, get it over with if you're going to."

He'd looked at his watch about five times in the last three minutes and he acted as if he expected someone or something. Ordinarily, a stupid punk like this, with orders to kill a man, simply does what he's told. I should have been dead minutes ago. A ray of hope was born. Slim enough to hide behind a thread, but I hadn't had even that a second before.

"All in good time," he said. "Hell, you ain't in a rush to get knocked off, are you?"

I started using propaganda again. A man with a gun poking his nose has no other weapon. "The blonde is stringing you. She doesn't go for mugs like you, Spike. I know, because I talked to her a little while ago."

"So maybe you made her, huh?"

I think if I'd said yes, he would have blown my fool head off. I said, instead, "She can't see me either. We're small fry in her book."

"Small, hell," he said. "She likes my build."

I couldn't stand it any longer. "What are you waiting for? Is there going to be an audience?"

He smiled that killer's smile again. "I think you are scared. Yeah, I bet your knees are shaking. Anyway, I wouldn't be a sucker and shoot. Somebody would hear that. All I'm going to do is bust you up in little pieces—quiet. If you yell, I'll wring your goddam neck. And I'll do it when I get good and ready."

So he didn't intend to use the gun. That wasn't his think-ing—somebody had warned him a shot could be easily heard in a hotel and maybe the place would be difficult to get out of. In that thick skull of his, the idea was strongly planted. If only I had a break, any kind of a break, he'd hesitate before pulling the trigger. Maybe he wouldn't even pull it at all. A break—just one little break. He glanced at his watch again.

"It ain't going to be long now, pal," he said. "I'm being fixed up with an alibi. In a minute or two, a friend of mine is going to call here. You're going to answer the phone. That'll prove you was alive at—" He looked at his watch again—"exactly twelve-fifteen. And if the cops take me for the job. I'll prove I was some place else at twelve-fifteen. Smart, ain't it?'"

A minute or two. That was all I had left.

The phone rang. It clamored. It sounded as if the bells were installed inside my head. It rang so loud the instrument and its base should have jumped all over the table. Spike didn't even glance at it.

"Okay, pal, answer it and don't try no tricks. Hurry up, I ain't got all night."

I had a lifetime. A very brief lifetime. I moved toward the phone.

CHAPTER THIRTEEN

"PICK IT UP," he said.

I reached for the phone, and he pulled the gun back, holding it aside a bit. I wasn't covered, but he could move that gun back into position so fast I wouldn't have been able to much more than lift a finger.

I said, "Hello."

"How you feeling, Sloan?"

It was a man's voice. It should have been familiar, but it wasn't. I didn't happen to be in a mood to recognize voices at that moment.

I said, "All right, I guess."

"Yeah—wait'll Spike starts working you over, boy. This is Paul Stoker. Remember me?"

I muttered something, then took the phone away from my ear, glanced at Spike. "He wants to talk to you."

Spike reached for the phone with his left hand. That put his right just below the phone I was still holding—and he was gripping the gun with that hand. He had orders not to shoot. He wouldn't, unless it was absolutely necessary. Well, he was going to have to shoot in about one second, but would he hesitate long enough? There was one way to find out. It might cost me my life, but that was forfeit, anyway.

I let the phone slide down until my fingers were clutching the end of it and I brought this down as hard as I could against Spike's right wrist. The blow must have paralyzed his finger nerves for a few seconds. Either that—or the command not to shoot held back the proper functioning of his brain, which should have been flashing a message to pull the trigger.

At the same instant I threw up my left hand and sent his head back. Then I brought up a knee, using all my strength. He went deathly pale, and the gun tumbled to the floor. He tried to yell but was in too much pain. He made a half punch, half grabbing gesture toward me, and I waltzed out of the way. I knew he'd snap out of it quickly enough, so I bent down and grabbed the gun. I rapped him with the muzzle just over the eyes. Blood spurted, blinding him. He turned away, groaning now, spread-legged, so pale that the blood seemed redder than it really was. I lifted the gun, holding it by the barrel and brought it down on top of his skull with every ounce of force I could muster. It must have been enough though you couldn't have proven it by me— not right then. All I knew was that I had to knock this man out, even kill him, or I'd die under a barrage of blows and kicks.

Spike went down on his knees. I clouted him again with the gun butt and he fell on his face. I picked up the phone. Nobody was on the wire. I hurried to the bathroom and found some adhesive tape. I started peeling it off, but the stuff was old and dry. It wouldn't hold Spike for more than a minute. I went back with a roll of sterilized gauze. I turned him over on his stomach, pulled his left hand behind him and untangled his right from under his body. I lashed the wrists with half the roll of gauze and tied a tight knot. Then I felt better. I started walking toward a chair, but I didn't quite make it. My knees gave way, and I had to grab at the edge of a table for support. Spike was beginning to groan. I sat down and lit a cigarette and wondered what the hell I was going to do with him.

Whatever came into mind had to be done fast. Paul Stoker knew something had gone wrong. This gang of hoods, ostensibly controlled by Maxine, might even dare to storm this fashionable hotel. Then I had a happy thought. I arose slowly, testing my legs before I put much weight on them. I was still clutching the gun.

Spike, if he got free of that gauze and tape, was going to get one smack through his chest if he came at me. I wasn't buying any more of that.

I picked up the phone and asked the girl on the switchboard to get me Police Headquarters. I asked for Captain Kane. The chances were he wouldn't be there, but, on the outside chance he was, I wanted him. He was there—and I cursed him silently. Sheila had been so afraid he'd be home early.

I said, "This is Mike Sloan, Captain."

He said, "Yes," as if his mouth was full of hot buckshot.

"Have you found the murderer of Marty Carroll yet?"

"I wouldn't tell you if we had," he said curtly. "Furthermore, I don't even want to talk to a lousy bastard like you."

"You'd better send someone else up here then, because I've got Marty's killer sprawled out on my floor and I hate to have my place cluttered up."

I dropped the phone, hoping it banged in his ear. He'd come. Kane wouldn't pass up a chance like this.

While I waited, Spike woke up. He gave some mighty tugs at the gauze, and I wasn't sure the stuff would hold so I went over to him, bent down and laid the muzzle of his gun against the tip of his nose.

"How does it feel, Spike?"

He called me a few names I was familiar with, a few I hadn't heard in years and some that were absolutely new to me.

"Stop squirming around," I said. "If you do bust the stuff holding your wrists, I'll only shoot you."

"Next time," Spike said, "I won't wait. I'll give it to you on sight."

"There won't be a next time, Spike. They may have trouble fitting you into the electric chair, but they'll manage. You killed Marty. You told me so, remember? And I'm betting you left enough prints around to tie you in even without the confession. How do you feel, pal?"

"Lousy. Would you listen to a deal?"

"The only deal you know is a double-cross. I'm sorry, Spike. I'm as sorry as hell."

"You buzzed the cops, huh?"

"I called Captain Kane."

"Kane, huh? Listen, wise guy, I'm not in any death cell yet. I'm telling you now—you'd better go far away and dig yourself a deep hole because I'm looking for you the minute I get out."

"You worry me, Spike."

He cursed some more and then lay back with his mouth wide open. He had yellow stumps for teeth. I wondered what he chewed to make them that yellow. He rolled his head to look at me again.

"I got me a few grand stashed away, pal."

"You'll need it for lawyers."

"Damn you. Listen, Paul Stoker knows something happened. He'll get you for me."

"I can handle Stoker. I did once already. Got any more bright ideas?"

He had some. They weren't bright—but they were very dirty. There was a pained silence for a while, and then somebody banged on the door. I took a firmer grip on the gun, turned the latch, put my back against the wall just inside the door and said, "Come in."

Kane threw the door wide as he always did. I lowered the gun just a trifle and peered over his shoulder. There was nobody in the corridor. I kicked the door shut, but I didn't put the gun away. Kane went over and stood looking down at Spike.

"This him?" he asked.

I said, "No, that's a special friend who just dropped in. He likes to lie around that way."

"You don't have to be a smart alec, Sloan. Who is he?"

"Spike Tate, a cheap hood with big muscles. He told me he killed Marty Carroll."

"In front of witnesses?"

"Hell no, but you could get the truth out of him. You couldn't detect his brain under a microscope. Besides, there must have been prints."

"How do you know?" Kane turned on me fast.

I'd made a mistake there. I wasn't supposed to have been at the scene of the crime. I said, "There were gory details in the newspapers, Captain."

"Prints," he said. "Yeah—there were prints. Of big thumbs and fingers. Cut him loose, Sloan."

"It's on your own head," I warned.

"While you're at it, give me that rod. Is it yours?"

"I took it away from him. I'll give it to you as you leave, Captain. You and I are not exactly friends."

"This is police busines," he said harshly. "Get him up."

I hauled Spike to his feet. It was impossible to untie the knots in the gauze because he'd pulled them too tight, so I got a pair of scissors from a table drawer.

"Wait a minute," Kane said. He stepped in front of Spike and slugged him on the mouth. It was a hard, vicious blow. Spike's frog eyes jumped wide open in surprise. Blood began trickling down over his chin.

"That's a sample of what you'll get if you make a break," Kane warned. "Okay, Sloan, free him."

I snipped the gauze. Spike brought his hands around to the front and started massaging his wrists. Kane turned to me.

"Drop down to my office in the morning. By then I'll have this bird singing sweet. The department thanks you. I don't Come on, you oversized chunk of blubber."

He pushed Spike toward the door. I said, "Easy, Captain. Take it easy."

"Who are you to give me orders?" he flared. "As a private citizen, you turned a prisoner over to me. I'll handle him the way I see fit."

"You'd better put cuffs on that guy," I said. "I'd hate to have him break your neck, Captain. Think of all the money I'd lose in that law suit."

Kane shoved Spike again. The big man offered no resistance. He never said a word, but at the door he turned around and glared at me. I broke his gun, ejected the slugs into my hand and gave the gun to Kane.

"Not that I don't trust you, Captain, but if I was found with a slug from this rod in me, you could say Spike did it. A slug from your own gun—you'd have a hard time explaining that one. Good night, Captain."

He shoved Spike again. I closed the door softly on them, double locked it, staggered over to a chair and sat down. I stayed there about two seconds, bobbed up again and carried the whole decanter of whisky back to the same chair. I guzzled it in mouthfuls. I couldn't even taste the stuff.

Gradually the fuzz cleared out of my brain. I gave a short, unhappy laugh. Kane was a smart guy. Very, very clever. He hadn't even asked me what Spike was doing in my suite. Now I knew what Kane was.

I got ready for bed, not moving very fast. The whisky had taken a secure grip and the glow felt good, but sometimes I didn't gauge things quite right. Like squeezing shaving cream on my tooth brush and laughing like hell over it. I was pleasantly plastered. Just the thing to begin a new life. It was a new life. I'd been dead forty minutes ago.

The phone rang as I was getting into my pajamas. I made it without spilling any furniture or falling on my face. Captain Kane's voice came over the wire.

"Sloan? No need to come to the office in the morning."

I said, "No? What'd he do, tell all?"

"I was taking him back in my car and he made a break for it. I killed him."

I didn't say another word. I hung up slowly and I was as sober as the Chairwoman of the W.C.T.U.

And I'd thought I knew what Captain Kane was! I was a fool. I didn't have as many brains as Spike had owned and I used them less. I went to the bedroom, turned down the covers and slid between the sheets. Usually I liked to lie there with the light on and think. Tonight I just lay there in a semistupor.

The light was still on when I woke up the next morning.

CHAPTER FOURTEEN

I WENT TO the office after a late breakfast, and the first thing I did was open the vault, take out the .45 and check its ammunition. I made sure there was a slug in the firing chamber and the safety worked easily. With this heavy artillery in my hip pocket, I felt a great deal better.

What I came to the office for I had no idea, except that it must have been done by sheer force of habit. I had nothing to sell even if a customer came in, and certainly I wasn't interested in buying. It was a quiet place, good for thinking. I did a lot of it, mostly about Sheila. I did wonder what had happened to Mona, and I was half tempted to call her apartment. However, the chances were good that I had enough trouble without starting any more. It was shortly after one o'clock when the phone rang for the first time and startled me almost as much as if it had been a bomb. I wasn't especially surprised at the voice which greeted me.

"Sloan, this is Maxine."

I said, "Good—I was wondering how I could get in touch with you."

"I understand you took very good care of Spike."

"I did what I had to do, baby. He was in good health when Captain Kane took him out of my suite."

"Do you think he's the only man in our organization, Sloan? Do you think you're quite safe now?"

"No, I don't. That's why I wanted to get in touch with you. I'm wide open and I know it. I can't go to the cops without involving myself, and so—when I'm faced with something I can't fight, I join in. That's what I want to talk to you about."

"Good," she said and her voice dropped to a purr. "We'll forget about what happened to Spike. He was a stupid beast anyway. I'll want to see you soon, Sloan."

"Make that Mike," I said. "If we're going to be partners, we might as well be friends."

"All right, Mike. Shall I come to your office tonight?"

"Oh, no. Not this time. I'm coming to see you, preferably at your home, but, wherever it is, we must be alone. I do my best talking when there's only one person present."

"I don't know about that, Mike."

"What's the matter, don't you trust me?"

"Yes, I suppose I must. All right. Take down this address. It's Elizabethan Towers—Maxine Hewitt. I'll expect you about eleven tonight."

"I'm looking forward to it, Maxine."

"So—am I." She hung up rather quickly.

I went to a movie that afternoon to kill time. Around seven I drifted into my favorite bar and grill, had a steak and plenty of trimmings. I took my time and ordered drinks after the meal was cleared away. Sheila came in around eight-fifty. I crossed the floor in her direction, didn't give a damn who saw me and kissed her soundly. She turned a pretty pink but linked her arm under mine. I took her back to the table. We sat down, I ordered more drinks, raised my eyes and stared.

"What's wrong, darling?"

"You have a new necklace, Sheila."

She fingered the single slim strand and smiled. "You have competition, Mike. Jack gave me this today."

"Your husband?"

She nodded. "It's a strange situation, Mike. Understand, there is nothing changed between you and me. But when I think back—when I realize how Jack used to be. He'd bring me little things—not necklaces, of course. Then he was promoted, and gradually he changed. A necklace wouldn't bring back the love he threw away. Not after I'd met you."

"That looks like a pretty good string of pearls," I said. "I'm in the business, and I ought to know. May I see it?"

She reached up and opened the catch. "Of course, Mike. I'd like to know how good it is. Jack said it was a bargain he stumbled on. You know—I'd hate to think he gave me something cheap to get back into my affections."

I ran the pearls through my fingers. "He wasn't a cheapskate, is that what you're trying to tell me?"

"Yes, that's it. Remember, I'm talking about the man I married. The old Jack. If I made a mistake judging him, then I'd never trust myself again."

"Meaning with me?"

She looked frankly at me. "Yes, Mike. I know so little about you now. Much less than I did about Jack. And I do know that you've been a—a crook. It doesn't matter. Not what's in the past. You've changed, too, but for the better. Not the way Jack changed. If I'd made a mistake in him as he used to be, it would hit me hard."

I said, "These are worth about four thousand dollars, baby."

"Four thousand? Then they are real?"

I nodded. "Pearls are tricky to judge. You have to be an expert, and I learned the business long ago. Where'd he get them?"

"I don't know. I suppose he did a favor for someone. He did say they cost him a lot of money, but he felt he ought to do something for me."

"Very nice of him." I handed the beads back. "Do you think he knows about us and this is his way to win you back?'

"No, Mike," she smiled. "He hasn't the faintest idea. And I'm ready now—if you are. I know exactly what I'll say in my letter to Jack."

I took out my handkerchief, touched it to my lips and then idly patted my forehead. I didn't want her to see the beads of cold sweat I knew must be there. I drank my drink too fast and wanted more. I called the waiter over and pointed to my empty glass.

"We'll be ready to leave in a day or two," I said. "We're going to a town about two thousand miles from here. I read in a trade journal that there is an old established jewelry store for sale, and I contacted the owner. He's an old man and anxious to get out. His terms are good; I can swing them with no trouble. It's a city of a quarter of a million people. I hope that's okay."

She laid her hand on mine. "Anywhere, darling, so long as I can begin life over again with you."

"We'll be living in sin, baby."

She shook her head. "Not with our kind of love. Some day we'll find out how Jack feels about this. Perhaps I can get a divorce. I don't care. I have you and nothing else matters."

"Those are words I'll remember," I said softly. "Is there any danger of Jack coming home unexpectedly tonight?"

"No, he called me. He may not be home at all. Something happened—another killing, I suppose."

"Yes," I said in a dry voice, "a killing—maybe."

She put her elbow on the edge of the table, cupped her chin in her hand and looked at me. "Tell me more about this city—this jewelry store."

We talked for about an hour and a half. She was so damned good for me. All the jitters I had went away meekly. I felt rested and at ease. I walked her back toward her apartment and took her into a doorway for a good long kiss. She liked that.

I said, "It won't be much longer, baby. I'll close up the office tomorrow or the next day, and then we'll be ready. Which reminds me, I'd better be on my way. There's a great deal to be done."

She put her cheek gently against mine. "I wish there was a lot for me to do. It would make the time pass faster. Kiss me once more, darling. I'll meet you again tomorrow night if things go right."

"Don't take any chances," I implored. "Not at this stage of the game."

She raised her face for a kiss. "I won't. I promise."

We held the kiss as long as we could. Then I stood there and watched her walk toward her apartment house. As she turned into the lobby, she looked back and waved. I just stood there thinking that if I disappointed her now, she'd never get over it. I'd have to be very, very careful. I thought about the pearl necklace, too. More than I wanted to.

I had to walk a couple of blocks before I picked up a cab, and I gave the driver Maxine's address. On the way, I remembered what the Elizabethan Towers were like. You didn't live there unless you had a roll—and a thick one with plenty more being added all the time. I had a few moments of doubt. What if Maxine really did run this racket by herself? With maybe a couple of backers who stayed out of sight. I'd be making a god-awful mistake. One I couldn't possibly rectify.

Could I have misjudged that blonde for a cheap, round-heeled tart when she was really smart enough to organize and control a gang with men like Spike and Paul Stoker ready to do her killing when she snapped her fingers? The doubts kept pushing at me, worrying me. I sweated again, worse than when Shelia showed me that necklace. I could be walking straight into the jaws of a big trap, and, if I sprung it, they'd find one Michael Sloan floating in the river after a couple of days. If there was enough left of me to float.

A flunky in the uniform of Queen Elizabeth's day saluted smartly as he opened the cab door. I wasn't sure if I was supposed to salute back, hand him a tip or just walk on by. I walked by.

More men in similar uniforms manned the elevators. This was a real formal joint.

I had to phone Maxine's apartment first and get her okay to come up. It was a warm, inviting okay. I started feeling a bit anxious as the high speed elevator shot upwards. From here on, until I rode down again, conventions were off. Sheila must be forgotten. I had a job to do and I wondered if it wouldn't be just a bit more pleasant than I'd anticipated.

She opened the door as I took my finger off the buzzer and she was especially prepared for me. She wore a long robe of some kind. It was baby blue and set off that blonde hair perfectly. It would have done better if the blondeness had been real. The gown may have been ankle length, but it certainly wasn't neck high. She was bare skin from her chin right down to her cleavage.

"My, my," I said with an approving leer, "no wonder you can run an outfit as you do. The boys must fall all over themselves to work for you."

She didn't answer, just twitched her hips over to a yellow chair and sat down. I put my hat on a table, took a seat opposite her and relaxed. She reached over to a metal cigarette box, found it empty and refused one of mine. Instead she went to the table where my hat lay, pushed it aside and picked up a leather hand-bag. She opened this and took out a pack of Turkish cigarettes. When she got one going, she crossed her legs and gave me a long, steady stare.

"I don't think I like you, Sloan. I know I don't like what you did to Spike."

I said, "I gave him a break, baby. I could have killed him, but I turned him over to the cops. If he chose to make a break for it, that's his own fault."

"Just the same..." she began to argue.

I cut her short. "Spike was going to murder me. I'd have been a true sap if I just stood there and let him do it. Now get this—if you want me to work for you, say so. If you don't, I might as well go home."

She smiled then, for the first time. "We'll get nowhere arguing. I need you and you need me. Shall we talk about a little job I have in mind?"

"I listen much better with a glass in my hand, Maxine."

She balanced the cigarette on an ash tray. "I'd like a drink myself. Excuse me."

She walked out of the living room, and as she disappeared I got up quietly, went over to the table and opened her handbag, a large, navy blue bag made of leather. Sewn to the inside of it was a holster containing a .32 automatic. Outside of the gun there wasn't anything in the bag to interest me, and I felt disappointed. What I was after was something leading to the guy she worked for. Somebody had set her up in this game, used her as an attractive front. I was back in my chair before she returned with a tray of ice cubes, glasses, ancient brandy and a bottle of sparkling water.

I fixed a pair of strong drinks, carried them to a divan, sat down and waited for her to join me. She laughed and sat down, accepting the drink and imbibing half of it quickly, as if she'd wanted a drink badly. I draped my right arm over the back of the divan, a couple of inches above her shoulders.

"I'm in the mood to listen now," I said.

"Good. We'll get along, Mike, and make a lot of money. You won't be sorry you joined us. I understand you're pretty clever at slipping a necklace off a woman's neck."

"I've done it without being caught," I said modestly.

"Tomorrow night the Metropolitan season begins. You know what that means."

I nodded. "All the worthwhile rocks in town will be there."

"Among them, the famous emerald necklace owned by Mrs. Suzette Perreau."

I laughed. "Every crook in town has been shooting at that for years. If you expect me to just walk up and grab it, think again. The opening night is attended by all the cops on the jewelry detail, as well as private guards."

Maxine finished her drink and sat holding the glass, rotating it slowly between both hands. I let my arm drop down a bit until my fingers touched her bare shoulder. If she knew it, she paid no attention.

"It will be done this way, Mike. As Mrs. Perreau steps out of her car, there'll be a big crowd. There always is. In that crowd will be about ten of my boys. They'll start shoving and pushing, maybe create a mild riot. You'll be as close to Mrs. Perreau as you can get. When the crush begins, your job is to whisk that necklace off. All you have to do then is squeeze your way to the curb. The boys will try to make a path for you. There'll be a car waiting. Get in, and that's all there is to it."

I had some of my drink and nodded slowly. "Not bad, Maxine. Not bad at all. An organization does help, at that. I think it'll work."

"Of course it will." She gave a delicious little shiver as I passed my fingers along her shoulder and then down her back. She suddenly pulled herself forward. "We ought to have another drink, Mike."

I said, "Sure," got up and went over to the table where she'd set down the tray. It was a large table. On it was a telephone and a phone number record book lying open. As I mixed the drinks, I looked down at it and flipped over a couple of pages when she couldn't see me do it. Under "M" I found a number. There was no name with it. There didn't have to be. I knew that number well. It belonged to Mona Montinez. I carried the drinks back to the divan.

I asked, "How many carats do the Perreau emeralds run, baby?"

"Carats? I—don't know for sure."

"And has it a diamond clasp?"

"I suppose so. What the hell, we'll know by this time tomorrow night, Mike. Let's stop talking shop."

I put the glass on the floor and my arm around her as I straightened up. "Suits me. So do you, beautiful. You suit me just fine."

She leaned back, pulled my hand down and pressed it against the first swell of her breast. I bent my head and kissed her in the middle of her throat. At close range it was like crepe instead of sweet young skin. Suddenly she dropped the empty glass she held. It rolled under the divan, but neither of us paid any attention to it. Her arms went around my neck, her lips moved toward mine.

I kissed her hard. At first, I didn't care much whether I did or not, but with the second kiss I started to care. I could tell by the way she breathed and the way her lips moved under mine that she felt the same way. She eased herself down so that she was lying across my lap, and she pulled her legs up onto the divan. I caressed an ankle, bent to kiss her again and stroked the nylon-clad curves of her calves. She made me hold that kiss a long, long time by wrapping an arm around my neck.

We came up for air after a while. I thought I might as well get something out of this. I cared nothing for her, except what she meant at this particular moment, and I wouldn't have hesitated to double-cross her.

I said, "Baby, you're wonderful."

"Better than other girls you've known, Mike?"

She was putting herself in a class with girls. I could have laughed in her face. "Better," I said, "than anyone. Maxine, do you know why I finally agreed to join your outfit? Not because I was threatened. Hell, I can take care of myself. But I knew it would give me a chance to know you better. Like now. Like this…"

I grabbed her hard and did some fancy work with the elastic that held up the gown. It slid down easily enough. I buried my cheek against the softness of her and I could hear her heart beating wildly. I grinned to myself. This wouldn't be too hard. What

I wanted to know were facts about who set her up. One man, two or three? In time, she might even tell me who he or they were. I didn't have any time.

She pushed me away for a moment, got to her feet and shook off the gown. Then she came back to me. I was in no hurry, but she seemed to be.

I said, "Maxine, we can't have just this one night and then forget all about it. We're alike, you and I. Exactly alike. We know what we want and we take it. We're smart, too—that scheme for getting the emeralds is perfect, and I'll show you I can pull it. But hell, I'd rather not get that necklace if it means losing you."

"Why should it mean losing me?" she asked in a low, hot voice.

"You told me once that there were important men behind you. Maybe these men won't like the way you play around with the hired help."

"To hell with them. What they don't know ..."

I fumbled with the hooks at the small of her back, got them open. My temperature soared. This woman was really built.

"But men who handle an outfit like this can be dangerous. Especially if there are several of them."

"I said to hell with them. Kiss me, Mike. Why do you keep up this damn chatter?"

I kissed her, a long one accompanied by gentle stroking of her back. She had her eyes tightly closed now, giving way to my lead, waiting for me.

I put my lips near her ear. "You and I could run this outfit and be together all the time. We wouldn't have to split with any-one except the chumps who work for us, and they'd get little. We'd be rich. Your talent for organization, my skill in doing the actual work. Baby, we'd go far."

She opened her eyes. "Mike, I'd like that."

"These men backing you—can they be taken care of?"

A flicker of suspicion robbed her eyes of some of the warmth which had been in them. "Are you trying to pump me, by any chance?"

I grinned at her. "Hell, no. I don't want any names. Just a word from you about whether or not we could stand our ground and defy them if it came to that."

She snuggled up to me again. "When I'm with you, Mike, he can go to the devil. I'm not afraid of anything."

He! One man—just as I thought. That was all I wanted to know. I should have tossed her on her fancy behind and left then, but it would have been a tip-off to her. Quite possibly she wasn't even aware of the fact that she'd given away some important information.

She strained against me, no longer wanting to be denied. I moved her into a sitting position and got up to turn out the lights. On my way back to the divan, in darkness, I paused long enough to slide my .45 under the cushions of a chair.

She wasn't on the divan when I reached it. She was standing, waiting to direct me to one of the doors off the living room.

That icy blonde exterior was only a fraud, a protective front for a warm nature that made pulse and temperature pound and boil. If I hadn't met Sheila, I might have gone for Maxine. She was something you didn't turn down easily.

CHAPTER FIFTEEN

I TIPTOED OUT of her apartment, retrieving my gun on the way. I closed the door softly so as not to awaken her and looked at my watch when I was in the lighted corridor. It was two-thirty. I reached the lobby, passed through it and hit the street. Four blocks away, I found an all-night drug store, bought some cigarettes and went to the phone booths. I called Sheila's number, the first time I'd ever done so. If Kane answered, I'd merely hang up.

But it was Sheila, and her voice was foggy with sleep. I said, "It's Mike. Can you talk?"

"Yes. Mike, what's wrong?"

"Not a thing. I just wanted you to know that we'll be moving tomorrow night. Very late—but tomorrow."

"Mike, that's wonderful."

"You're all alone?"

"Yes—Jack hasn't come home yet."

"Meet me about ten or eleven at our usual place tomorrow night. We'll make our plans then. Okay?"

"I'll be there, darling."

I said, "I just found out something. I love you very, very much. Good night."

I hung up quickly. There were many things to be done. Maxine had given me the tip I needed. I knew where I stood. How this would all turn out was problematical and everything that would happen from here on was replete with danger, but it had to be faced. I scouted up a taxi and had the driver take me to Mona's apartment house.

It was like entering familiar territory. I'd been there so often and yet it seemed so long since the last time. There were public phone booths in the far corner of the lobby. I entered one and dialed Mona's number. It took her quite a while to answer, but, unlike Sheila's, her voice wasn't sleepy.

I said, "This is Mike. Now don't hang up, for Christ's sake. I'm calling from the office and I'm coming around to see you right now."

"Mike, you damned fool. It's three in the morning."

"I don't care what time it is. I have to see you. Expect me in about ten minutes."

I hung up before she could argue the point, but I didn't leave the phone booth. I could see the elevators from where I stood in the cubicle, but I knew I couldn't be seen. About six minutes went by and then the self-service car, used after midnight, came to the lobby floor and the door opened. Captain Jack Kane came out in a big hurry. He was trying to knot his tie as he rushed toward the exit. I knew the answer all right. The few remaining doubts I had vanished now. I gave him ten minutes, and then I walked out. I hoped Mona would worry herself sick over me.

At home, I undressed and climbed into bed, lying there with the light on. I wasn't tired, even though it had been a busy day and tomorrow night might be even busier. All the little things were falling into place. Like the way Captain Kane had turned on me at the Fairweather party and searched me for the second time. I'd wondered then what was behind that. Now I knew. He'd been looking for the little necklace snipper I'd invented. If he had found that, he'd have had a case, as open and shut as though I'd carried a kit of burglar tools. Of course, Mona had told him about it—and more. Mona was the reason why Kane didn't come home to Sheila until very late, if he came home at all.

Then there was the attack when I left the Fairweather party. That had to be set up beforehand. I'd tried to think who could have been so sure I'd have the pearls. Now I knew Mona would have figured I'd be smart enough to get them even if Kane and his boys were present. Kane wouldn't have rigged it by himself. He was too cocksure, but Mona knew me, and she'd been taking no chances.

That hot temper of Mona's had boiled over when we met the last time. From me, she'd gone straight to Kane with the whole story. And Kane had trusted her, confided to her that he was checking into the rackets. As a ranking cop he knew all the ropes. He even had Maxine to front for him, knowing very well how a good-looking, well-stacked blonde could hold the boys in line. Kane meant to put every jewel thief, fence and fingerman under his thumb.

It was all so clear now that I cursed myself for not seeing the details long ago. The truth had come only in driblets; now it was all added up, stacked and ready for use. First of all, Marty Carroll had just about admitted Kane warned him not to do any more business with me. Then Marty had changed his mind and asked me to come back. He'd even intended to buy merchandise from me. What had made him change his mind so abruptly? Somehow he discovered that Kane was backing a new outfit intent on taking over all the lush jewelry business in town. Marty was the kind of man who'd hate a crooked cop even though he was a crook himself. So Marty had died because he defied Kane. So had at least one other gem thief who couldn't see any reason why he should turn over most of his profits to an organization he didn't need.

Kane had murdered Spike. I should have known Kane wouldn't dare lock Spike up. The big dumbbell would have talked under pressure. Yet Kane was in no position to let him go, so he must have told Spike to run for it and make it look good—and then he'd shot him in the back. I think I hated Kane more now than I ever had.

A cop who goes wrong is nothing new. I'd seen them come and go. Some were high-class crooks, but rarely did one of them ever possess the nerve to set up a gang that he was, as a police-man, supposed to wipe out. It would have worked for a while, too. It would still work if I was out of the picture, and I thought that was in Kane's plans for me.

Another idea hit me. A disturbing one. If Mona told Kane all about me, she must have included the fact that I was in love with Sheila. Kane was fully capable of murder. He'd kill Sheila before he'd let me get her. Maybe he wouldn't even wait. I swung my legs off the edge of the bed on an impulse to go for Sheila now—shoot my way clear of Kane, if necessary. Then I settled back. Kane wanted me first and foremost. He'd do nothing to upset his plans for that. Sheila was perfectly safe—for the present.

It was after five when I drifted off to sleep, after ten when I woke up. I had plenty of time. I packed a bag first, took it to the office and put it in the back room out of sight. Then I visited my safe deposit vault and cleaned out the box. Securities, cash and gems went into a big briefcase. I put this into the office safe. I was ready now for a quick trip.

Around four o'clock, I telephoned Inspector McDermott and finally convinced him it would be a good idea to meet me. He showed up at the corner I designated, and I took him for a ride through the park in my car. McDermott was no fool. He listened long and well. I didn't feel like a stool pigeon. I was getting out of the rackets, but I didn't want those who stayed in to be dominated by someone like Kane. I knew McDermott would take care of him. Cops hate crooked cops most of all.

McDermott kept what he thought of me to himself and went along with my plans. He let it drop that he, too, had suspected Kane.

He got out of my car a ten minute taxi ride from Head-quarters. That was at his suggestion. If we were seen together and Kane heard about it, everything might be off.

I had an early dinner in a restaurant near my hotel, returned to my suite and took my time getting into evening clothes. I surveyed myself in the mirror. I looked like any other well-groomed opera lover. I tested the little gadget for snatching a necklace until the use of it came back to me and I was proficient with the thing. I did plenty of thinking about Sheila, too, and several times I was tempted to call her. I gave up the idea because the risk would be too great.

Ready half an hour ahead of time, I sat down and had a stiff drink and a couple of cigarettes. One item bothered me. How would Sheila take it when she found out her husband was a worse crook than I'd ever been?

Yet I couldn't back down now. Maybe I could get her away before the story broke, prepare her so that if she eventually did learn the truth, she'd be able to face it. Her judgement of me wasn't mistaken. I'd changed for her. I was giving up stealing. Sure, the thrill of the profession gets in a man's blood. I'd miss it, but with Sheila beside me I could forget it, too. I shuddered with the thought that she might back out. My new life would be less than pointless without her. I'd have to go back to the rackets or die of boredom, and from here on I'd face many more risks than ever before if I began stealing again. McDermott was cooperating because he had to, but I knew he'd take me in ten minutes afterwards if he had anything on me.

It was time to go. I felt like someone walking to the electric chair.

I reached the entrance to the Met in plenty of time. There was a crowd around, as always. For some reason, people like to see all the splendor and glitter that passes through the doors. There were cops around, and I suspected there were a lot of detectives posted nearby, too. I didn't see any I knew, but then Inspector McDermott might have sent over only cops from other divisions, men he could trust.

My evening clothes opened up a path for me. I stood close to the curb, waiting. Cops weren't allowing any cars to park in the block, but Maxine would arrange that. With Kane planning the whole thing, it had to come off without a hitch.

At seven-thirty on the dot, Mrs. Perreau's limousine rolled up. The doorman let her out with a flourish. Behind her car was another, and in the back seat was Maxine, dolled up as if she intended to go inside, too. Things were going to move fast now. I reached for the little snipping gadget and began edging my way toward Mrs. Perreau.

She was rearranging her wrap. The emeralds around her neck glowed like green traffic signals. She started walking across the sidewalk, and then it began. Someone gave somebody else a shove. In about ten seconds the sidewalk was full of milling people. There were a lot of curses, a great deal of shoving. The whole thing worked so beautifully I had to mentally compliment Kane on his scheme.

If there were cops handy, they'd have a hard time getting through that tightly packed, jostling mob. I was right behind Mrs. Perreau. Somebody gave me a hard shove, and I bumped against her. I apologized and she looked at me, but I knew it was an involuntary gesture. She wouldn't have recognized me again. My face was just another in an angry sea of faces. I lifted the little gadget and brought it down again—and then the little clamps were holding a hundred and fifty thousand dollars' worth of emeralds.

I got them into my pocket swiftly. It had all taken about two seconds. I managed to turn around. Maxine's car was at the curb with the back door open and the doorman standing uncertainly by, pushed now and then by the milling crowd. Some uniformed cops were diving into the mess, making it worse. A big guy with mug written all over him opened a path for me. He didn't use his elbows. He used fists and feet.

I reached the car, got in and the big guy got in behind me. The door closed and the car slid smoothly away into the traffic. I didn't think Mrs. Perreau had even missed her necklace yet.

Maxine linked her arm under mine and moved very close to me. The big guy just sat there. The driver concentrated on the traffic and the man beside him merely looked me over, grunted and paid no more attention.

Maxine said, "You got it, Mike?"

I gave her a happy nod. "Sure."

She squirmed with pleasure. "Let me see it, Mike."

I shook my head. "Not now. Where are we going?"

"To a good spot. We'll be safe there. Do you think anyone recognized you?"

"No—and what if they did? Nothing could be proven. There's even a chance the cops won't know there was a theft until the opera is half over. I'm betting Mrs. Perreau doesn't know it yet."

Maxine was all smiles. "Think what we can do in this racket, Mike. There's no limit. Now do you see how right you were in joining us?"

I didn't see it at all, but I pretended I did. Nobody said anything while the car shot over to Broadway and continued on downtown. Pretty soon the traffic thinned. We took a right turn and went down a side street. When we were very close to the river, the driver slowed up and turned into a driveway between two warehouse buildings.

"Is this where we're headed?" I asked.

"That's right, Mike. One of these warehouses is empty. The boss took it over."

"Is he going to meet us?"

"I think so. You're going to be surprised, Mike. You're going to faint dead away when you see him."

The car stopped beside a loading platform. The big guy got out. I started to, but he suddenly grabbed me around the waist, hauled me out and held me while one of the other goons lifted the .45 out of my hip pocket. The big guy stuck the gun into my ribs.

Maxine climbed out. "Hey, what's the idea?" she demanded. "I didn't tell you to do this."

"Shut up," the big guy said. "I don't take my orders from you."

"Why, you lousy son of a—"

One of the other boys pushed Maxine away and grabbed my arm. I was half dragged, half carried onto the loading platform. Two more men were inside waiting. They had the door open. When it closed, I saw that we were in a huge empty room. The big guy gave me a shove that sent me reeling away until I lost my balance and fell. When I started to get up, he pointed my own gun at me.

"Stay there," he said sharply. He was no Spike Tate. This guy was almost as big, but he had brains to go along with his brawn. Maxine hopped around trying to find out what this was all about. Nobody paid any attention to her.

Finally she went over to a small window, brushed off a workbench directly beneath it and put her leather handbag down. Then she hoisted herself up and let her legs dangle. One of the men ogled her. So did I. This could be the last time I'd ever see a pair of fine legs.

They wouldn't let me move. I wrapped my arms around my knees, stayed on the floor and waited. A good fifteen minutes went by. Not a word was spoken. The ogler had a cigarette going, but it hung slack between his lips. He couldn't take his eyes off Maxine.

Finally she couldn't stand the suspense any longer. Her voice had gone shrill. "Will somebody tell me what this is all about? Mike swiped those rocks, didn't he? He's one of us. Why in hell do you treat him like that?"

"Shut up," the big guy said calmly. "Or I'll help you do it."

Maxine kept quiet, which was very wise. Another five minutes went by. Then the loading platform door opened and Kane walked in. He was alone, and smiling from ear to ear. Without a word he walked over to me and aimed a kick at my face. It missed, but I took it high on the arm, and it didn't feel good. I got to my feet. To hell with them all.

The big guy raised the gun as a club and moved toward me. Kane stretched out an arm and stayed him. "Not now, Barney. I want him to know what this is all about first."

I said, "I thought you were a cop. What is this?"

Maxine said, brightly, "I told you you'd be surprised, Mike."

Kane didn't even turn to glance at her. He said, "If that blonde opens her yap again, close it. Well, Sloan, I guess you are surprised, at that—but you haven't heard half of it. Sure I've gone into your line, but not in the cheap way you handled it. From here on, all the jewel thieves work for me. Go on, admit it. That was a smart set-up back there at the Met."

"I admit it," I said.

"It's nothing compared to the plans I have in mind. They'll make me rich, Sloan. I'll be stinking rich. After I get what I want, I'll resign from the force. My first million and I quit. I'm no hog."

I said, weakly, "Of course if I'd known, I wouldn't have made all that trouble for you. Lawsuit and all ... ."

"I'm not worried about it. In a little while, there won't be anybody to press the suit. Besides, you'll be found here nice and dead. I'll take the credit for your capture. Sure—I saw you around the Met, I saw you snip off the necklace and I trailed you. That'll prove you're nothing but a cheap, lousy crook. Where would your case be then—even if you were alive to push it?"

I had to stall. "Listen, Kane, we're on the same side now. I thought I was supposed to work for you."

"Do you actually think I'd trust a rat like you, Sloan? What would happen if I did? You'd be looking for a way out. Maybe you'd find it. Knowing I was a crooked cop would help. The least you could do would be to run for it—and take my wife with you. You goddam stinking rat."

I said nothing, but he didn't need any conversational help from me. He went right on. "I've known it for a long time. Your old girl friend told me. Well, at least I can thank you for her. We get along, Mona and I."

"What about Maxine?" I asked.

"She knows where she stands with me."

Maxine jumped off the bench, left her handbag there and walked up to stand beside Kane. There was hate in her eyes. "Are you telling me this guy was fooling around with your wife?"

"Sure," Kane said. "He swiped more than jewelry."

"Shoot him, Jack. Blow his damned head off. Do you know what that rat was doing? Conning me. Yeah—making me think I was the only dame in his life. Go on—plug him. What's keeping you?"

"He'll get it when I'm ready," Kane said. "Well, Sloan, how does it feel to be on the other end of a lot of trouble?"

"What happens to Sheila?" I asked him.

"I haven't made up my mind yet. I hate her guts, but throwing her out would only be doing her a favor. I'll keep her around. I'll remind her of you occasionally."

I said, "Kane, I know you're going to kill me. That's okay because, when I went into this business, my eyes were open. But that girl used to be in love with you. She told me so a dozen times. She said she married a swell guy who went sour somewhere along the way. If she thought you used to be good and decent, you must have been in love with her, too. Why must you crucify her? Think back to what you used to be. If you don't want her any more, let her go."

"You'd like that, wouldn't you? Maybe I should let you go, too, so the two of you could scamper off somewhere. I'll decide what to do about her later. I've already made up my mind about you, Sloan. Now hand over that necklace."

I reached into my pocket, took out the glittering green string of emeralds and watched them reflect the single overhead light. I started to hand them to Kane and stopped short. I brought them back and squinted closely at them. Then I began laughing.

"What the hell is wrong?" Kane yelled.

I kept on laughing. "This is too funny, Kane. It's the perfect finish to the goofiest business I was ever in. These things are phonies."

He yanked them out of my hand. "You're a liar. They're genuine."

"Okay, Kane, but wait until you try to sell them. I don't know why I should, but I can prove they're no good if you want me to."

"How?" He regarded me suspiciously.

"Hand them over," I said. He gave them to me reluctantly, but I could see that he was worried. "I'll prove it by crushing one of the stones just like the glass it is."

Nobody stopped me when I walked toward the workbench. I put the necklace down beside Maxine's purse. They were coming up behind me fast, but I had a chance to open the catch of the purse.

"Well, go ahead," Kane ordered. "If this is a trick, you'll be a hell of a long time dying, Sloan."

I said, "Lend me a knife."

Kane fished into his pocket and gave me one. I opened the small blade, bent over the bench and the necklace and pried one of the stones out of its setting. Then I hacked at it with the point of the blade. I picked up the loose stone and handed it to Kane.

"Take a look yourself. See the scratches, notice how deep they are. Now I'll loosen another stone and smash it if you need more proof."

He held the stone between his fingers and turned toward the light just as I knew he would. Maxine was at his side, the four hoods pressed close, worried that they'd been cheated out of a big cut. All I had to do was open Maxine's leather handbag, the same one I'd already examined at her apartment, and take out the gun it contained.

One of the men saw me. He let out a howl and reached for his pocket. I shot him through the face.

"Your gun, Kane," I said. "I'll shoot it out of your hand . . ."

He let go of it. The other two moved into line with Kane. They were nicely behaved boys. The guy on the floor without a face was a good example of what they'd turn into if they ceased being good boys.

I backed toward the door. "Maxine—you're coming with me."

She scampered away from the others. She got the door open for me and ran through. Maxine wasn't bright, but she knew the more space she put between herself and Kane, the happier she was going to be. The handy handbag and the gun looked like a frame-up on her part.

I slammed the door shut, leaped off the platform, raised the gun and fired two quick shots. Then I ran after Maxine. Kane came out on the platform and threw a couple of slugs my way, but he was too rattled to shoot straight. Then a searchlight from a nearby window in another building bathed him in its glare. He swore and ran back into the building.

Cops, uniformed and in plain clothes, moved in after Kane. Somebody inside smashed a window and started shooting through it. I saw one of the men outside fold up. Maxine, frozen in fear, didn't run when I joined her. The cops weren't doing any shooting yet, but the patrolman on the ground was groaning and trying to crawl away. Another bullet from that same window stopped him. I saw his body jerk as the slug hit and then he was very quiet.

There were more shots from inside, but oddly enough none of the other cops went down. There were yells and screams also and then half a dozen shots. They weren't being fired at anyone outside. You could tell by the reverberations from that massive empty room. Then, suddenly, the loading door opened and the big guy came crashing out, a gun in each hand. He must have been hit by twenty slugs. After that, there was just a lot of eerie silence.

I put my arm around Maxine. "Baby, this is where we part company. I'll stall for you. Get your stuff packed and blow. Move fast."

Her eyes lighted up. "Mike, you're coming with me?"

I said, "Not on your life. I've had enough of bums, but in a way you helped me, and you rate a break. Get going before I change my mind."

She didn't argue. She took off like a startled doe. I watched her disappear with a small sigh. She hadn't been so bad after all.

Then I saw Inspector McDermott come out of the warehouse. He spotted me and started over.

CHAPTER SIXTEEN

McDERMOTT AND I went into the first café we came upon. That it happened to smell of stale beer, cheap whisky and cheaper perfume didn't matter. We sat down at a table and ordered rye straight.

McDermott said, "Damned if I can understand the man. He died in there, Sloan. But he took three of those goons with him."

I nodded, tossed my drink down quickly. "There was something good in Kane, even tonight. Sure, he was going to shoot me down and laugh at me while I died, but I still say the guy wasn't all bad. Do you know what must have happened in there?"

"I think so. I'd like to know what you think, Sloan."

"Everything was okay so long as nobody got hurt. But when Kane saw a cop go down and try to crawl away and then saw one of his boys pump another slug into the wounded cop, Kane stopped being a crook and became a cop again."

McDermott nodded. "That's how I figured it. Well, what do we do now?"

"You're asking me?" I signaled for a repeat drink.

"It's kind of up to you, isn't it, Sloan?"

I said, staring straight ahead and seeing nothing, "Kane saw the job pulled and trailed the necklace here. He died in the line of duty. It would read nice in the papers."

McDermott said, "He had the necklace in his hand when we found him. The necklace in one hand, a smoking gun in the other and three lousy hoods plastered with his slugs."

"Two," I said. "I killed the one without a face."

"Trouble," McDermott said softly. "Trouble all around. Three hoods with Kane's gun."

"Three," I agreed.

"Mrs. Perreau gets her necklace back, a little busted up, but it can be fixed easy."

"A hundred and fifty thousand dollars' worth of green ice," I said. "Kane didn't know his gems. They're as real as he is dead."

"I don't get that, Sloan."

"You don't have to."

McDermott said, "Nobody saw you, Sloan."

"I wasn't even there."

"I'll tell it the way it looked to me. Okay?"

"That's how I'd want it, Inspector."

McDermott frowned and tossed down his second drink. "It would certainly be hell if somebody—some damn fool—ever tried to make people believe different."

I said, "I'm leaving town in a couple of days. I've had enough of this business."

"Good." McDermott pushed his chair back. "Read the newspapers, friend. It'll be fine reading. After all, he did do his best when the cards were down. Even if he dealt them crooked."

"Somebody ought to tell his widow. I know her. Let me take care of it, Inspector."

"Yeah—if your story jibes with what she'll see in the papers."

"That's exactly how it will be."

McDermott arose. "So long, Sloan. Stay out of town. I'd hate like the devil to see you hauled in."

We shook hands and walked out. On the street, he went one way while I called a taxi.

Sheila sat there dry-eyed and heard me through. "Kane was a fool to walk into that mess," I said. "I didn't know he had that much nerve. He saw these mugs swipe the necklace, tailed them and got the whole gang. Something must have slipped.

They got him, but he got three of them first. He stood there and fought it out. They're going to put his name high on the honor roll."

She got up to face me then, put her head on my shoulder and sobbed. I felt clumsy. All I could do was murmur vague words and pat her shoulder. Finally she drew back a little.

"I'm glad he went that way, Mike. He always thought he would. In the old days, he used to tell me not to cry too much if it happened. He must have had a premonition."

"Yes," I said, "a premonition. I shouldn't be asking this, but does it make any difference between you and me?"

She shook her head and her hair got into her eyes. I brushed it away tenderly.

"No, darling," she said. "You're my new life. I need you more than ever now."

What could I say? It was no time to express joy.

"You see, Mike, I was right. I didn't misjudge Jack. He'd changed, yes, but he was still the big roughneck I married. He had courage. It didn't fail him, and he didn't fail me."

"We don't have to hurry now, baby. Not like before, but I want to get started as soon as this is all finished. That store won't wait forever."

"I'll be ready when you are, Mike. I want to get away, too."

She came into my arms. I held her close with just one hand; the other dipped into my pocket and came out with the little snipping gadget. I sliced through the string of her necklace and when I stepped back, the whole thing slid down to the floor. With a little cry, Sheila bent down to gather up the pearls which had rolled off the string. I helped her.

"Give them to me," I said. "This will be my first job as an honest man. I'll restring them for you."

"Be careful of them, Mike. I know you won't mind if I keep them to sort of—well, remember what Jack was long ago. So long ago."

I dumped the beads into my pocket. "I'll have them for you tomorrow, Sheila. In a couple of days we'll settle everything and get started. I want that new life, too."

She managed a smile. "And we won't have to live in sin. Oh, Mike, it turned out for the best, didn't it? Even if it was—like—this."

She didn't mind when I left. She had a lot of remembering to do and even more anticipation of our future. I picked up a cab and had myself driven to my office.

I paid off the cab driver and stood at the curb until he pulled away, and then I walked to the corner. I took the beads out of my pocket, forced those still on the string free and dumped them all down into a sewer. A couple ran around the concave design of the sewer cover and I pushed them in with my shoe.

I went up to my office, took off my coat, removed the links from my dress shirt and rolled up the sleeves. I opened the big vault, took out my briefcase and carried it into the workroom. I switched on the light, straddled the stool and unrolled a piece of velvet in which were a couple of hundred fine pearls. I cut the clasp of Sheila's necklace free of its string, tied on a new string and started stringing it with my own pearls.

There might be a slight difference in the size of some of them, but I doubted that Sheila would notice. I knew exactly what her necklace had looked like. Why not? I'd made it up myself. It was the one I'd given Mrs. Brindley to wear home in place of her own. The same necklace which had been stolen from her.

That son of a bitch had found out from Mona that all his men had got for their pains was a phony, and he'd given it to Sheila. That was just like Kane. He was a phony all through.

I got the last pearl on finally. It had taken a long time and I was tired, but I stuck with it. I attached the clasp, made one piece out of the whole thing and held it up for a final examination. She wouldn't know the difference, but if she ever had it appraised, it would be worth about four grand.

The things a guy will do for a woman!